"It's really you I want to talk to," Samuel said.

"Me?" Anna's mouth gaped open and she snapped it shut. Her stomach turned over. "Something I can do for you?"

"*Ya.* I want..."

Anna shifted her weight and the wooden step under her left foot creaked.

"If you would..." He took a deep breath and straightened his broad shoulders.

Staring at him, Anna couldn't stop the fluttering in the pit of her stomach. "*Ya?*" she coaxed. "You want..."

"I want to court you, Anna," Samuel blurted out. "I want that you should give me the honor to become my wife."

Anna froze, unable to exhale. She blinked as black spots raced behind her eyes. Abruptly, she felt her hands go numb. Her knees went weak and the ladder began to sway. There was an ominous crack of wood, the step broke, and paint, ladder and Anna went flying.

Books by Emma Miller

Love Inspired

*Courting Ruth
*Miriam's Heart
*Anna's Gift

*Hannah's Daughters

EMMA MILLER

lives quietly in her old farmhouse in rural Delaware amid fertile fields and lush woodlands. Fortunate enough to be born into a family of strong faith, she grew up on a dairy farm, surrounded by loving parents, siblings, grandparents, aunts, uncles and cousins. Emma was educated in local schools, and once taught in an Amish schoolhouse much like the one at Seven Poplars. When she's not caring for her large family, reading and writing are her favorite pastimes.

Anna's Gift
Emma Miller

Love Inspired

Recycling programs
for this product may
not exist in your area.

LOVE INSPIRED BOOKS

ISBN-13: 978-0-373-81577-7

ANNA'S GIFT

www.LoveInspiredBooks.com

Printed in U.S.A.

Let your beauty not be external…but the inner
person of the heart, the lasting beauty of a gentle
and tranquil spirit, which is precious in God's sight.
—1 *Peter* 3:3–4

For Mildred,
for the delight her beauty brought to my world.

Chapter One

Kent County, Delaware...Winter

Anna Yoder carried an open can of robin's egg-blue paint carefully through the big farmhouse kitchen, down the hall and into the bedroom across from her mother's room. Her sister, Susanna, trailed two steps behind, a paintbrush in each hand.

"I want to paint," Susanna proclaimed for the fourth time. "I can paint good. Can I paint, Anna? Can I?"

Anna glanced over her shoulder at her younger sister, and nodded patiently. "Yes, you can paint. But not right now. I'm cutting in and it's tricky not getting paint on the floor or the ceiling. You can help with the rolling later."

"*Ya!*" Susanna agreed, and her round face lit up in a huge smile as she bounced from one bare foot to the other and waved the paintbrushes in the air. "I'm the goodest painter!"

Anna chuckled. "I'm sure you are the *best* painter."

Susanna was nothing, if not enthusiastic. Of her six sisters, Susanna was the dearest and the one toward which Anna felt most protective. Sweet, funny Susanna was the baby of the family and had been born with Down syndrome. Their Dat had always called her one of God's special children; at eighteen, Susanna still possessed the innocence of a girl of nine or ten.

Fortunately, for all the tasks that came hard to Susanna, such as reading, sewing or cooking, the Lord had blessed her with a bottomless well of special gifts. Susanna could soothe a crying baby better than any of them; she always knew when it was going to rain, and she had a rare ability to see through the complications of life to find the simple and shining truth. And sometimes, when things weren't going well, when the cow had gone dry or the garden was withering for lack of rain, Susanna could fill the house with laughter and remind them all that there was always hope in God's great plan.

Still, keeping track of Susanna and running the household was a big responsibility, one that Anna felt doubly, with Mam off to Ohio to bring Anna's grandmother, great aunt and sisters, Rebecca and Leah, home. Susanna and Anna would be on their own for several days. Their sister Ruth and her husband, Eli, who lived just across the field, had gone to a wedding in Pennsylvania. Irwin, the boy who lived with them, had accompanied their sister Miriam and her husband, Charley, to an auction in Virginia. Not that Anna didn't have help. Eli's cousin was pitching in with the milking and the outside chores, but Anna still had a lot to do. And not a lot of time to get it all done.

Anna had promised Mam to have the house spic-and-span when she returned home, and she took the responsibility seriously. Having both Miriam and Ruth marry and move out in November had been a big change, but bringing Grossmama and Aunt Jezebel into the house would be an even bigger change. Grossmama was no longer able to live on her own. Anna understood that, and she knew why her mother felt responsible for Dat's aging mother, especially now that he was gone. The trouble was, Grossmama and Mam had never gotten along, and with the onset of Alzheimer's, Anna doubted that the situation would improve. Luckily, everyone adored Grossmama's younger sister, Jezebel; unlike Grossmama, Aunt Jezebel was easygoing and would fit smoothly into the household.

"We're paintin' because Grossmama's coming," Susanna chirped. Her speech wasn't always perfect, but her family understood every word she said. "She baked me a gingerbread man."

"Ya," Anna agreed. "She did." Susanna was the one person in the household who her grandmother never found fault with, and that was a good thing. If Grossmama could see how precious Susanna was, she couldn't be that bad, could she?

Once, when she was visiting years ago, Grossmama had spent the afternoon baking cookies and had made Susanna a gingerbread man with raisin eyes, a cranberry nose and a marshmallow beard. Susanna had never forgotten, and whenever their grandmother was mentioned, Susanna reminded them of the gingerbread treat.

Grossmama had fallen on the stairs at her house the previous year, fracturing a hip, so Mam hadn't wanted her climbing the steps to a second-floor bedroom here. Instead, they'd decided to move Anna and Susanna upstairs to join Leah and Rebecca in the dormitory-style chamber over the kitchen. Grossmama and Aunt Jezebel could share this large downstairs room just a few feet away from the bathroom.

It was a lovely room, with tall windows and plenty of room for two beds, a chest of drawers and a rocking chair. Anna knew that Grossmama and Aunt Jezebel would be comfortable here...except for the color. Anna couldn't remember which of her sisters had chosen the original color for the walls, but Grossmama hated it. She'd made a fuss when Mam had written to explain the new arrangements. Grossmama said that she could never sleep one night in a bed surrounded by fancy "English" walls.

By saying "English," Anna understood that her grandmother meant "not Plain." To Grossmama, white was properly Plain; blue was Plain. Since the ceiling, the window trim, the doors and the fireplace mantel were white, blue was the color in Anna's paint can. Actually, Anna didn't see anything improper about the color the room was now. The muted purple was closer to lavender, and she had a lavender dress and cape that she really loved. But once Grossmama set her mind on a thing or against it, there was no changing it.

Standing in the bedroom now, staring at the walls, Anna wished Ruth was there. Ruth was a good painter. Anna prided herself on her skill at cooking, perhaps more than she should have, but she knew that her painting ability was sketchy at best. But, since the choice was between Susanna or her, Anna knew who had to paint the room.

Of course, she'd meant to get started sooner, but the week had gotten away from her. Susanna had a dentist appointment on Monday, which took all afternoon by the time they had to wait for the driver. On Tuesday, there had been extra eggs, which needed to go to Spence's Auction and

Bazaar. Normally, they didn't go to Spence's in the winter months, but Aunt Martha and Dorcas had opened a baked-goods stand. Anna had taken the opportunity to leave Susanna with their oldest sister, Johanna, so that she could go with Aunt Martha to sell her eggs and jams.

Now it was Wednesday. After Mam left at dawn, Anna and Susanna had spent the morning scrubbing, dusting, polishing and setting her yeast dough to rise. Now there were no more excuses. Anna had to start painting if she wanted to be finished on time. Because they were alone, Anna wore her oldest dress, the one with the blackberry stains, and had covered her hair—not with a proper white *kapp,* but with a blue scarf that Irwin's terrier had chewed holes in.

Knowing that Susanna would be certain to lean against a freshly painted wall, Anna had made sure that Susanna's clothing was equally worn. That way, if the dresses were ruined it wouldn't be a waste. Anna's final precaution was to remove her shoes and stockings and ask Susanna to do the same. Paint would scrub off bare feet. Black stockings and sneakers wouldn't be so lucky.

Gingerly setting the can on the little shelf on the ladder, Anna climbed the rickety rungs, dipped her brush in the can and began to carefully paint along the wall, just below the ceiling. She'd barely gone two feet when Susanna announced that she was hungry. "Wait a little," Anna coaxed. "It's still early. When I get as far as the window, we'll have some lunch."

"But, Anna, I'm hungry *now.*"

"All right. Go and fix yourself a honey biscuit."

"'Fff…thirsty, too," she said, struggling to pronounce the word properly.

"Milk or tea. You don't need my help."

"I'll make you a biscuit, too."

"*Ne.* I'll eat later. Don't wander off," she cautioned her sister. "Stay in the house." Susanna was capable of taking care of herself on the farm, but it was cold today, with snow flurries in the forecast, and she didn't always remember to wear her coat. It wouldn't do for Mam to come home and find Susanna sick with a cold.

Anna continued to paint. The blue covered the lavender better than she thought it would. It would need a second coat, but she had expected as much. As she carefully brushed paint on the wall in a line along the ceiling's edge, Anna began to hum and then to sing one of her favorite *fast tunes* from the *Liedersammlung.* She liked to sing when she was alone. Her voice wasn't as good as Johanna's or Ruth's, but singing made her feel bubbly inside. And now, with only Susanna to hear, she could sing as loudly as she wanted. If she was a bit off-key, her little sister wouldn't complain.

"Anna? Maybe we come at a bad time?"

Startled by a deep male voice, Anna stopped singing midword and spun around, holding onto the ladder with her free hand. "Samuel!"

Their nearest neighbor, the widower Samuel Mast, stood inside the bedroom holding his youngest daughter, Mae, by the hand. Mortified by her appearance and imagining how awful her singing must have sounded, Anna wanted to shrink up and hide behind the paint can. Of all the people to catch her in such a condition, it had to be Samuel Mast. Tall, broad-shouldered, handsome Samuel Mast. Anna's cheeks felt as though they were on fire, and she knew she must be as flame-colored as a ripe tomato.

"I remembered what you said." Susanna hopped from one foot to the other in the doorway. "I didn't go outside. Let Samuel and Mae in." She beamed.

"You're busy," Samuel said, tugging on Mae's hand. "We can come back another—"

"*Ne,*" Anna interrupted, setting her brush carefully across the paint can and coming down the ladder. "Just…you surprised me." She tried to cover her embarrassment with a smile, but knew it was lopsided. *Samuel.* Of all the people to see her like this, in her patched clothing and bare legs, it had to be Samuel. Her stomach felt as though she'd swallowed a feather duster. "It's not a bad time," she babbled in a rush. "I'm painting the room. Blue."

"*Ya,* blue. I can see that." Samuel looked as uncomfortable as she felt. Anna had never seen him looking so flustered. Or untidy, for that matter. Samuel's nut-brown hair, which badly needed cutting, stuck out in clumps and appeared to have gobs of oatmeal stuck in it. His shirt was wrinkled, and one suspender hung by a thread. Even his trousers and shoes were smeared with dried oatmeal.

"Something wrong?" Anna glanced at Mae. The child was red-eyed from crying, her nose was running, her *kapp* was missing, and her face and hands were smeared with dried oatmeal, too. Anna's heart immediately went out to the little girl. She'd left her aunt's only two weeks ago, to live with her father for the first time, and Anna knew the move couldn't have been easy for her. "Are you having a hard morning, pumpkin?"

Mae's bottom lip came out and tears spilled down her cheeks. "Want…want Aunt L'eeze. Want…want to go home! Want *her!*"

Anna glanced at Samuel, who looked ready to burst into tears as well, and took command. "Mae—" she leaned down to speak to her at eye-level "—would you like to go with Susanna into the kitchen and have a honey biscuit and a cup of milk?"

Mae nodded, her lower lip still protruding.

Anna stood up. "Susanna, could you get Mae a biscuit?"

"Ya," Susanna agreed. "And wash her face." She smiled at Mae. "You look like a little piggy."

For seconds, Mae seemed suspended between tears and a smile, but then she nodded and threw her chubby arms up to Susanna.

Samuel sighed as Susanna scooped up Mae and carried her away. "I don't seem to get anything right with her," he said.

Anna smiled. "Best to *feed* children porridge and *wash* them with soap and water. Not the other way around."

Samuel returned a hint of a smile, obviously embarrassed. "It's…been hard…these last weeks," he stumbled. "Having her home. She's been four years with my sister, and I'm…we're strange to her. She doesn't know me or her brothers and sisters."

Sensing that it might be easier for Samuel to share his concerns if she continued with her work, Anna climbed the ladder again and dipped her brush into the can.

Aunt Martha had been telling Mam the other day that Samuel was finding it difficult to manage his farm, his house and to care for five children, and that it was just a matter of time before he realized it. *"Then* he'll start looking for a wife," she'd said. "Something he should have done three years ago."

"When Frieda passed, little Mae was only two months old," Samuel continued. "I had my hands full, so Louise thought it better if she took the baby home to Ohio until…until…"

Anna knew *until* what—until Samuel finished mourning his wife and remarried. Usually, widowers waited a year before looking for a new partner, but sometimes, when there were small children, the waiting period might be much shorter. Samuel's widowerhood had somehow stretched to four years.

In all those years, Samuel had made no formal attempt to court anyone, but most of Kent County suspected that he was sweet on Mam. Despite their age difference—Mam was eight years older—it would be a fine match. Samuel was handsome, a deacon of the church, and would make an excellent provider for an extended family. Not only did their farms run side-by-side, but Samuel had one of the finest dairy herds in the state.

Everyone liked Samuel. It wasn't just that he was a good-looking bear of a man, with his broad shoulders, a sturdy build and warm brown eyes, but he was hardworking, funny and fair-minded. It was clear that he and Mam were good friends, and Samuel spent many an evening at their kitchen table, drinking coffee, talking and laughing with her. Why he hadn't formally asked to court her, Anna couldn't guess. But that was okay with Anna. It was hard for her to imagine having Samuel for a stepfather. She'd secretly dreamed about him, although she'd never said a word to anyone other than her cousin, Dorcas. Even now, just having him in the room with her made her pulse race and her head go all giddy.

Anna knew, of course, that Samuel Mast, probably the catch of the county, would never look at her. Anna considered herself sensible, dependable, hardworking and Plain. But among the pretty red-haired Yoder sisters, Anna stuck out like a plow horse in a field of pacers. A healthy mare, her Aunt Martha called her, but no amount of brushing her hair or pinching her cheeks could make her pretty. Her face was too round, her mouth too wide, and her nose was like a lump of biscuit dough.

Her mother had always told her that true beauty was in the heart and spirit, but everyone knew what boys liked. Men were attracted to cute girls and handsome women, and it was the slender *maedles* with good dowries who got the pick of the best husband material.

No, Anna wasn't foolish enough to consider ever marrying a man as fine and good-looking as Samuel, but it didn't keep her from dreaming. And it didn't stop her from wishing that there was someone like him somewhere, who could see beneath her sturdy frame and Plain features, to appreciate her for who she was inside.

"Don't worry," Aunt Martha always said. "Any woman works as hard as you do and cooks *hasen kucha* like yours, she'll find a man. Might be one not so easy on the eyes out West someplace, or a bucktoothed widower with a dozen sons and no daughters to help with the housework, but someone will have you."

Anna knew she wanted a husband, babies and a home of her own, but she wondered if the price might be higher than she wanted to pay. She loved her mother and her sisters, and she loved living in Seven Poplars with all the neighbors and friends who were dear to her. She wasn't certain she would be willing to leave Delaware to marry, especially with the prospects Aunt Martha suggested would be available to her.

"Anna?"

"Ya?" She glanced back at Samuel, feeling even more foolish. While she'd been dream-weaving, Samuel had been saying something to her. "I'm listening," she said, which wasn't quite true.

"My Frieda is dead four years."

Anna nodded, not certain where the conversation was going. "She is," Anna agreed. "Four years."

"And two months," Samuel added. "Time I… made plans for my family."

Suddenly realizing what he might be talking about, she grasped the ladder to keep it from swaying. "I'm sorry you missed Mam." Her voice seemed too loud in the empty room. "I'm not sure when she'll be home. A few days. It depends on the weather and how Grossmama is feeling."

"I…didn't come…didn't come to speak…to Hannah." Each word seemed to come as a struggle.

She paused, resting her brush on the lip of the paint can, giving him her full attention. If he hadn't come to talk to Mam, why was he here? Was he sick? Was that why he looked so bad? "Do you need help with something? Charley should be back—"

"*Ne.* It's you, really, I want to talk to."

"Me?" Her mouth gaped open and she snapped it shut. Her stomach turned over. "Something I can do for you?"

"*Ya.* I want…"

Anna shifted her weight and the wooden step under her left foot creaked. "You want…" she urged, trying to help.

"If you would…" He took a deep breath and straightened his shoulders.

He was a big man, so attractive, even with his scraggly hair and oatmeal on his clothes. He filled the doorway, and staring at him, Anna couldn't stop the fluttering in the pit of her stomach. *"Ya?"* she coaxed. "You want…"

"I want to court you, Anna," Samuel blurted out. "I want that you should give me the honor to become my wife."

Anna froze, unable to exhale. Surely he hadn't

said what she *thought* he said. She blinked as black spots raced before her eyes. Abruptly, she felt her hands go numb. Her knees went weak and the ladder began to sway. An instant later, paint, ladder and Anna went flying.

Chapter Two

"Anna!" Samuel rushed forward in an attempt to catch her, and they went down together in a crash of wood, entwined arms and legs, and what seemed like gallons of blue paint. Samuel slid rather than fell to the floor and ended up with Anna in his lap, his arms securely around her middle. Somewhere in the jumble, the paint can hit the wall and bounced, spraying paint everywhere.

Samuel peered into Anna's startled face. Her eyes were wide, her mouth gaped, but the only sound she made was a small, "Oh, no."

"Are you hurt?" he asked, letting go of her when he realized he still held his arms tightly around her. He tried to rise, slipped in the river of paint and sat down hard, a splat rising from around his britches. As they fell a second time, Anna's arms instinctively went around his neck, bringing her face only inches from his. She was so close, he could have kissed her full, rosy lips.

"Anna?" he said, out of breath. "Are you all right?"

She gave a gasp, wiggled out of his embrace and scrambled up, her back foot slipping. Throwing both arms out for balance, she caught herself before she went down again.

Samuel knew he had to say something. But what?

Anna sucked in a gulp of air, threw her apron up over her blue-streaked face and ran through the doorway, nearly running into Susanna and Mae, and out of the room.

"Anna," he called, trying to get to his feet again, but having less luck than she had. "Come back. It's all right." He dropped onto all fours and used his hands to push himself up. "It's only paint. Anna!"

But Anna was gone, and the only evidence that she'd been there was the warm feeling in his chest, and a trail of bright blue footprints across the wide, red floorboards.

"You spilled the paint." Susanna began to giggle, then pointed at him. "And you have paint in your beard."

"Beard," Mae echoed, standing solemnly beside her newfound friend.

Samuel looked down at his blue hands and up

at the two girls, and he began to laugh, too. Great belly laughs rolled up from the pit of his stomach. "We did spill the paint, didn't we?" he managed to say as he looked around the room at the mess they'd made. "We spilled *a lot* of paint."

"A lot," Susanna agreed.

Mae stared at him with her mother's bright blue eyes and clutched the older girl's hand. The fearful expression in his daughter's wide-eyed gaze made him want to gather her up in his arms and hug her, but in his state, that was out of the question. Two painted scarecrows in one house was enough; the hugs would have to wait until later.

"Susanna, could you go and see if your sister is hurt?" Samuel asked. His first instinct was to follow Anna to see for himself that she was okay and to assure her that she had no need to be embarrassed. Anyone could have an accident, and the wooden ladder had obviously seen better days. But he'd heard her run up the stairs, and it wouldn't be seemly for him to intrude on her. With her mother out of the house, he had to show respect and maintain proper behavior. If he was going to court Anna, he was going to do it right and behave the way any man courting her would be expected to.

"Ya," Susanna agreed. Still giggling, she trotted off with Mae glued to her skirts.

Turning in a circle, Samuel exhaled and wiped

his hands on his pants. The way he'd been swimming in the paint, they were a total loss anyway. He rubbed a bruised elbow and the back of his head as he studied the floor, the wall, and the broken ladder. How, he wondered, had so much paint come from one gallon?

This was a fine barrel of pickles.

After putting it off for so long and practicing his proposal of marriage to Anna over and over in his head, it had gone all wrong. It couldn't have gone worse. He didn't know what he'd expected, but he certainly hadn't thought the statement of his intentions would frighten her so badly that she'd fall off a ladder, or drop into his arms—although that had been a pleasant interlude. He didn't know why sweet Anna had been so surprised, or why she'd run away from him. He hoped that it wasn't because the idea of marrying him and instantly becoming the mother of five children was so preposterous.

Samuel picked up the paint can and set it upright—there couldn't have been more than half a cup of paint left in the bottom. The room was a disaster. He decided he'd better get a start on cleaning it up before the paint began to dry. If he was lucky, maybe Anna would come down and join him and they could talk. He would need rags, a mop and maybe even a shovel to start wiping up the excess paint, but he didn't have the faintest idea where to find them.

The first thing he needed to do, before he went looking for the supplies, was to take his shoes off so he didn't track paint through the house. Setting the ladder upright, he sat down on the lower rung and began to unlace his brogans.

Samuel wondered if he'd gone about this all wrong. The custom was for the suitor to ask a go-between to talk to the girl's family before a proposal of marriage was formally offered. But with Anna's father dead and not a single brother, that left Hannah as the sole parent. Samuel supposed he could have approached Anna's uncle by marriage, Reuben Coblentz, but that would have involved Reuben's wife, Martha. Reuben didn't scratch until Martha told him where he itched. Plus, Hannah and Martha didn't always see eye to eye, and Hannah had made it clear that she didn't care for her late husband's sister interfering in her personal family matters.

That left speaking directly to Hannah before he approached Anna, but he'd decided against that because he was afraid that Hannah might have misconstrued his previous regular visits to the Yoder farm. There wasn't any doubt in Samuel's mind that most of the community thought that he was courting Hannah, or at least testing the waters. It could well be that Hannah thought so, too, and he didn't want to make matters worse by embarrassing her, maybe even hurting her feelings. Samuel liked Hannah, and he always enjoyed her company, but there was no comparing the warm friendship that he felt for her to his keen attraction to Anna.

What Samuel and his late wife, Frieda, had had was a comfortable marriage, but his father and her family had arranged the match. Samuel had been willing because it seemed such a sensible arrangement. He thought Frieda would make a good wife, and he'd always been reluctant to go against his father's wishes.

He'd been just nineteen to Frieda's twenty-three when they wed. Everyone said that it was a good match, and he could remember the excitement of their wedding day. Neither of them had expected romance, but they'd come to respect and care for each other, and they both adored the children the Lord sent them.

When Frieda's heart had failed and he'd lost her, he'd genuinely mourned her passing. But Frieda had been gone a long time, so long that he sometimes had trouble remembering her face. And he was lonely, not just for a helpmate, not just for a mother for his children, but for someone with whom he could open his heart.

If he was honest with himself, Samuel reckoned he'd been attracted to Anna for at least two years. Just seeing her across a room gave him a breathless, shivery thrill that he'd never experienced before. Oh, he wasn't blind. He knew what the other young men in the community thought about Anna. She wasn't small or trim, and she didn't have delicate features. Some fellows went so far as to make fun of her size. Not where Anna could hear, of course, or him either. He would have never stood by and allowed such a fine woman to be insulted by foolish boys who couldn't see how special she was.

In his heart, Samuel had always admired strong women. Other than Frieda, who'd been the exception, every girl he'd ever driven home from a singing or a young people's gathering had been sturdy. His mother, his sisters and his aunts were all good cooks and mothers, and all of formidable size. Like Anna, they all had the gift of hospitality, of making people feel welcome in their homes. And regardless of what anyone else thought, he appreciated Anna Yoder for who she was. "Big women have big hearts," his father always said, and Samuel agreed.

For longer than he wanted to admit, Samuel had been watching Anna and trying to convince himself that it was just his loneliness. After all, how fair was it for a man with five children and the responsibility of a large farm to propose marriage to a beautiful young woman like Anna? So he'd put off the decision to do anything about his feelings. As long as he didn't speak up, he was free to imagine what it would be like having her in his house, sitting beside him at the kitchen table, or bringing him a cold glass of lemonade when he was hot and sweaty from working in the fields. Month after month, he'd waited for her to reach the age of twenty-one, but when she had, he still hadn't found the nerve to ask.

What if she rejected him out of hand? So long as he didn't speak up, he could keep on going to Hannah's house, sitting at their table, savoring Anna's hot cinnamon-raisin buns and chicken and dumplings. But once he brought up the subject, if Anna refused him, Hannah might have no choice but to discourage his visits.

He hoped he was a truly faithful man, a good father and a good farmer. He'd been blessed by beautiful children, caring parents and a loving family. The Lord had provided material goods, land of his own and a fine herd of dairy cows. He served on the school board and helped his neighbors. His life should have been full, but it wasn't. He longed for Anna Yoder to be his wife.

It had taken his sister Louise to finally put an end to his hesitation. She'd brought Mae home, handed her over, and told him that it was time he found a new wife and a new mother for his children. He had to agree. It was past time. But now that he'd made up his mind and chosen the right woman, he'd made a mess of things.

What must Anna think of him? No wonder she was embarrassed. He'd had his arms around her, had her literally *in his lap,* and they'd both been doused in blue paint, like some sort of English clowns. He wanted to court her honorably, to give her the love and caring she deserved, and instead he'd made her look foolish.

In his stocking feet, Samuel stepped over a puddle of paint, taking in the room again.

After the mess he had made, it would serve him right if Anna never spoke to him again.

Anna stood in the shower in the big upstairs bathroom and scrubbed every inch of her skin. She knew that she should be downstairs cleaning up the terrible mess she'd made, but she couldn't face Samuel. She'd probably have to hide from him for the rest of her life.

How could she have been so clumsy? Not only had she fallen off the ladder, but when Samuel had tried to catch her, they'd both gone down in a huge pool of blue paint.

She wished she could weep as her sisters did, as most girls did when something bad happened. But this was too awful for tears. Not only had she embarrassed herself and Samuel, but she'd probably ruined things between her mother and

Samuel. She'd be the laughing stock of the community, and Samuel would probably never come to the Yoder farm again. And all because of her foolish daydreaming. What a silly girl she was, thinking Samuel had said he wanted to court her. She probably needed to clean out her ears. She had obviously misunderstood.

"Anna!" Susanna cracked the bathroom door. "You made a mess."

"Go away," Anna ordered.

"Samuel told me to come see if you were all right."

"He didn't leave yet?" her voice came out a little shrill.

"Nope. He told me to come see if you—"

"I'm fine," Anna interrupted, hugging herself. Emotion caught in her throat at the sheer mention of Samuel's name. "Just go away, please."

The door opened wider, and her sister's round face appeared. Anna could see her through the filmy, white shower curtain.

"Are you blue, Anna? Will the blue come off? Will you be blue on Sunday? At church?"

"Susanna! I'm in the shower." Eli had promised to fix the lock on the door a few weeks ago when he'd put the doorway in between the room over the kitchen and the upstairs hallway in the main house, but he hadn't gotten to it. She'd have to remind him

because right now there was no privacy in the upstairs bathroom. "I'll be out in a minute."

"But Anna…"

"Anna," repeated little Mae.

Susanna had brought Mae to the bathroom!
Anna took a breath before she spoke; there was no
need to take this out on Susanna. It was all her own
fault. "Take Mae back downstairs to her father. See
them out. And give them some biscuits!"

Without waiting for an answer, Anna turned the
hot water knob all the way up and stood under
the spray. *Give Samuel biscuits?* Had she really
said such a thing? Was there no end to her foolishness? Samuel didn't want her biscuits. After the
way she'd embarrassed him, he'd probably never
again eat anything she baked.

Anna could hear Susanna and little Mae chattering in the hall and she felt trapped. If Mae was
still in the house, Samuel had to be. She couldn't
possibly get out, not with him still here.

"She has to go potty," Susanna piped up over
the drone of the shower. "Mae does. She has to go
bad."

Gritting her teeth, Anna peered around the
shower curtain. The water was beginning to get
cool anyway. They had a small hot water tank that
ran on propane, but there wasn't an endless supply
of warm water. "All right. Just a minute. Close the
door and let me get dried off." She jumped out of

the shower, grabbed a towel and wrapped it around herself. "All right, Susanna. Bring Mae in."

Susanna pushed open the door. "There's the potty, Mae."

"Do you need help?" Anna asked the child.

Mae shook her head.

Anna wrapped a second towel around her head. "When she's done, wash her hands, then her face. Clean up her dress and bring her into the bedroom. We can fix her hair." She smiled down at the little girl. "Would you like that? I never pull hair when I do braids. You can ask Susanna."

"Anna does good hair braids," Susanna agreed. "But I fink she needs a bath," she told Anna. "She looks like a little piggy."

A quick examination of the little girl convinced Anna that she wasn't all that dirty, she'd just lost a battle with her breakfast. "We don't have time for a bath. I'm sure Samuel needs to be on his way."

Susanna wrinkled her nose as she looked at the little girl. "You spill your oatmeal this morning?"

"*'Frowed* it. It was yuck," Mae said from her perch.

Susanna's eyes got big. "You *throwed* your oat-meal?"

"*Ya.* It was all burny." She made a face. "It was lumpy an' I *'frowed* it."

On her father as well, Anna realized, suddenly feeling sympathy for both father and daughter.

"Well, don't do that again," she admonished gently, tightening the big towel around her. "It's not polite to throw your breakfast. Big girls like Susanna never throw their oatmeal."

"Ne," Susanna echoed, helping the little girl rearrange her dress. "Never." She turned to Anna. "Are you going to court Samuel?"

Anna gasped. "Susanna! What would make you ask such a thing?"

"Because Samuel said—"

"Were you listening in on our conversation, Susanna?" Anna's eyes narrowed. "You know what Mam says about that."

"Just a little. Samuel said he wants to court you."

"Ne," Anna corrected. "You heard wrong. Again. That's exactly why Mam doesn't want you listening in."

That, and because Susanna repeated everything she heard, or *thought* she heard, to anyone who would listen. Obviously, she had misheard. They'd both heard wrong. That was why Anna had lost her balance and fallen off the ladder. She'd misunderstood what Samuel said. There was no way that he wanted to court *her*. No way at all. She was what she was, the Plain Yoder girl, the healthy girl—which was another way of saying fat. But was it really possible that they had both misheard?

More possible than Samuel wanting to court her!

Anna hurried out of the bathroom. "Bring her in as soon as I'm decent."

She dashed down the hall to the large bedroom over the kitchen and quickly dressed in fresh underclothing, a shift, dress and cape. She combed her wet hair out, twisted it into a bun and pinned it up, covering it with a starched white *kapp*. A quick glance in the tiny mirror on the back of the door showed that every last tendril of red hair was tucked up properly.

The few moments alone gave her time to recover her composure, so that when the girls came in, she could turn her attention to Mae. *Please let me get through this day, Lord,* she prayed silently.

When Susanna and Mae came into the bedroom, Anna sat the child on a stool and quickly combed, parted and braided her thin blond hair. "There. That's better." She brushed a kiss on the crown of Mae's head.

"She needs a *kapp*," Susanna, ever observant, pointed out. "She's a big girl."

"*Ya,*" Mae agreed solemnly. "Wost my *kapp*."

"Find me an old one of yours," Anna asked Susanna. "It will be a little big, but we can pin it to fit."

In minutes, Mae's pigtails were neatly tucked inside a slightly wrinkled but white *kapp,* and she was grinning.

"Now you're *Plain*," Susanna said. "Like me."

"Take her downstairs to her father," Anna said. "Samuel will be wondering why we've kept her so long."

"You coming, too?" Susanna asked.

Anna shook her head. "I'll be along. I have to clean up the bathroom." It wasn't really a fib, because she did have to clean up the bathroom. But there was no possibility of her looking Samuel in the eye again today, maybe not for weeks. But she couldn't help going to the top of the stairs and listening as Samuel said his goodbyes.

"Don't worry, Samuel," Susanna said cheerfully. "Anna wants to court you. It will just take time for her to get used to the idea."

"Court you," Mae echoed.

What Samuel said in reply, Anna couldn't hear. She fled back to the safety of the bathroom and covered her ears with her hands. She should have known that her little sister would only make things worse. Once Susanna got something in her head, it was impossible to budge her from it. And now Samuel would be mortified by the idea that they all thought he wanted to court her instead of Mam.

Anna stayed in the bathroom for what seemed like an hour before she finally got the nerve to venture out. She might have stayed all morning, but she knew she had to clean up the paint before it dried on Mam's floor. She would have to mop up everything and get ready to start painting again tomorrow, after she and Susanna went into town to get more paint. The trip itself would take three hours, beginning to end.

Anna wasn't crazy about the idea of going to Dover alone in the buggy; she liked it better when Miriam or Mam drove. She didn't mind taking the horse and carriage between farms in Seven Poplars, but all the traffic and noise of town made her uncomfortable.

By the time Anna got downstairs, she'd worked herself into a good worry. How was she going to get all the painting done, tend to the farm chores and clean the house from top to bottom, the way she'd hoped?

Calling for Susanna, Anna forced herself down the hall toward Grossmama's bedroom. She pushed opened the door and stopped short, in utter shock. The ladder was gone. The bucket was gone, and every drop of paint had been scrubbed off the floor and woodwork. The room looked exactly as it had this morning, before she'd started—other than the splashes of blue paint on the wall and the strip she'd painted near the ceiling. Even her brushes had been washed clean and laid out on a folded copy of *The Budget*.

Anna was so surprised that she didn't know whether to laugh or cry. She didn't have to wonder who had done it. She knew. Susanna could never have cleaned up the mess, not in two days. Anna was still standing there staring when Susanna wandered in.

"I'm hungry," she said. "I didn't get my lunch."

Anna sighed. "*Ne.* You didn't, did you?" She glanced around the room again, trying to make certain that she hadn't imagined that the paint was cleaned up. "Samuel did this?"

Susanna nodded smugly. "He got rags under the sink. Mam's rags."

"You mustn't say anything to anyone about this," Anna said. "Promise me that you won't."

"About the spilled paint?"

"About the spilled paint, or that I fell off the ladder, or the mistake you made—" she glanced apprehensively at her sister "—about thinking Samuel wanted to court me."

Susanna wrinkled her nose and shifted from one bare foot to another. "But it was funny, Anna. You fell on Samuel. He fell in the paint. It was funny."

"I suppose we did look funny, but Samuel could have been hurt. I could have been hurt. So I'd appreciate it if you didn't say one word about Samuel coming here today. Can you do that?"

Susanna scratched her chubby chin. "Remember when the cow sat on me?"

"*Ya,*" Anna agreed. "Last summer. And it wasn't funny, because you could have been hurt."

"It was just like that," Susanna agreed. "A cow fell on me, and you fell on Samuel. And we both got smashed." She shrugged and turned and went out of the room. "Just the same."

Exactly, Anna thought, feeling waves of heat wash under her skin. *And that's how Samuel must have felt—like a heifer sat on him.* Only, this cow had thrown her arms around his neck and exposed her bare legs up to her thighs like an English hoochy-koochy dancer.

If she lived to be a hundred, she'd never forgive herself. Never.

Chapter Three

The following morning proved cold and blustery, with a threat of snow. All through the morning milking, the feeding of the chickens and livestock and breaking the thin skim of ice off the water trough in the barnyard, Anna wrestled with her dread of venturing out on the roads. She needed to buy more paint, but she didn't know if it was wise to travel in such bad weather. The blacktop would be slippery, and there was always the danger that the horse could slip and fall. And since she didn't want to leave Susanna home alone, she'd have to take her, as well.

Anna considered calling a driver, but the money for the ride would go better into replacing the paint. If only she hadn't been so clumsy and wasted what Mam had already purchased. She wondered if she could find some leftover lavender paint in the cellar. If there was any, maybe she could cover the blue splashes, and put the room back as it had been.

But the truth was, Grossmama would be angry if she found her new bedroom *English purple,* and Mam would be disappointed in Anna. Anna had caused the trouble, and it was her responsibility to fix it. Snow or no snow, she'd have to go and buy more blue paint.

What a noodlehead she'd been! Was she losing her hearing, that she'd imagined Samuel had said that he wanted to court her? She tried not to wonder how Susanna could have misheard, as well. It was funny, really, the whole misunderstanding. Years from now, she and her sisters would laugh over the whole incident. As for Samuel, Anna thought she'd just act normal around him, be pleasant, pretend the whole awful incident had never happened and not cause either of them any further embarrassment.

After the outside chores, Anna returned to the house, built up the fire in the wood cookstove, and mixed up a batch of buttermilk biscuits while the oven was heating. Once the biscuits were baking, she washed some dishes and put bacon on. "Do you want eggs?" she asked her sister.

"Ya," Susanna nodded. "Sunshine up." She finished setting the table and was pouring tomato juice in two glasses, when Flora, their Shetland

sheepdog, began to bark. Instantly, Jeremiah, the terrier, added his excited yips and ran in circles.

"I wonder who's here so early?" Anna turned the sizzling bacon and pulled the pan to a cooler area of the stove.

Susanna ran to the door. "Maybe it's Mam and Grossmama."

"Too early for them." Thank goodness. Not that she wasn't eager for Mam to get home. Her younger sisters had been away for nearly a year, with only short visits home, and she'd missed them terribly. But Grossmama would make a terrible fuss if her room wasn't ready and the walls were still splashed with blue paint.

Susanna flung open the door to greet their visitor, and the terrier shot out onto the porch and bounced up and down with excitement, as if his legs were made of springs. Coming up the back steps was the very last person on earth Anna expected to see. It was Samuel, and he'd brought his three daughters: five-year-old Lori Ann, nine-year-old Naomi and Mae, all bundled up in quilted blue coats and black rain boots. They poured through the door Susanna held open for them. The two older girls carried paint rollers, and Samuel had a can of paint in each hand.

"It's Samuel!" Susanna shouted above the terrier's barking. "And Mae! And Naomi! And Lori Ann!"

Anna's stomach flip-flopped as she forced a smile, wiping her hands nervously on her apron. "Samuel." She looked to Naomi. "No school today?"

She pushed her round, wire-frame glasses back into place. "My tummy had a tickle this morning, but I'm better now."

"I think we were missing our teacher," Samuel explained. "I let her stay home. She never misses. Do I smell biscuits?" He grinned and held up the paint cans. "We didn't mean to interrupt your breakfast, but I wanted to get an early start on those walls."

Confused, Anna stared at him. "You wanted to get an early start? You bought paint?"

"Last night." He smiled again, and mischief danced in his dark eyes as he set the cans on the floor. The girls added the rollers and brushes to the pile. "I just took my shirt along to the store, and they were able to match the color perfectly."

"Good you brought paint," Susanna announced. "Now we don't have to take the buggy to town."

"I don't know what to say." Anna gripped the front of her apron. "It's kind of you, but you have so much to do at your farm. We'll pay for the paint, of course, but—"

"I smell something burning." Naomi peered over her glasses and grimaced.

Anna spun around to see smoke rising from the stove. "Oh, my biscuits!" She ran to snatch open the oven door, and used the hem of her apron to grab the handle of the cast-iron frying pan.

"Be careful," Samuel warned.

A cloud of smoke puffed out of the oven, stinging Anna's eyes. She gave a yelp as the heat seared her palm through the cloth, and she dropped the frying pan. It bounced off the open door, sending biscuits flying, and landed with a clang on the floor. Anna clapped her stinging hand to her mouth.

Lori Ann squealed, throwing her mitten-covered hands into the air, and the terrier darted across the floor, snatched a biscuit and ran with it. In the far doorway, the dog dropped the biscuit, then bit into it again, and carried it triumphantly under the table. Flora grabbed one, too, and ran for the sitting room with her prize.

"They're burned," Naomi pronounced, turning in a circle in the middle of the biscuits. "You burned them, Anna."

"Never mind the biscuits, just pick them up," Samuel said. Somehow, before Anna could think what to do next, he had taken charge. He crossed the kitchen, retrieved the cast-iron frying pan from the floor using a hand towel, and set it safely on top of the stove. "How bad is the burn?" he asked as he put an arm around her shoulders, guiding her to the sink. "Is it going to blister?"

"I'm all right," Anna protested, twisting out of

his warm embrace. Her palm stung, but she was hardly aware of it. All she could think of was the sensation of Samuel's strong arm around her and the way her knees felt as wobbly as if they were made of biscuit dough.

Samuel gently took her hand in his large cal-loused one, turned on the faucet, and held her palm under the cold water. "It doesn't look bad," he said.

"Ne." Anna felt foolish. How could she have been so careless? She was an experienced cook. She knew better than to take anything out of the oven without a hot mitt.

"Let the water do its work." Samuel said, speak-ing softly, as if to a skittish colt, and the tenderness in his deep voice made Anna's heart go all a-flutter again. "The cold will take the sting away."

"Does it hurt?" Susanna asked.

Anna glanced at her sister. Susanna looked as if she were about to burst into tears. *"Ne.* It's fine," Anna assured her. Susanna couldn't bear to see anyone in pain. From the corner of her eye, Anna saw Mae raise a biscuit to her mouth. "Don't eat that," she cautioned. "It's dirty if it's been on the floor."

Samuel chuckled, picked up a handful of the biscuits and brushed them off against his shirt. "A little scorched, but not so bad they can't be sal-vaged," he said.

"In our house, we have a five-second rule,"

Naomi explained, grabbing more biscuits off the floor. "If you grab it up quick, it's okay."

"Mam says floors are dirty," Susanna said, but she was picking up biscuits as well, piling them on a plate on the table.

Anna knew her face must be as hot as the skillet. Why was it that the minute Samuel Mast walked in the door, she turned into a complete klutz? She hadn't burned biscuits in years. She always paid close attention to whatever she had in the oven. She wished she could throw her apron over her face and run away, like yesterday, but she knew that she couldn't get away with that twice.

"Don't put them on the table," Anna said. "They're ruined. I'll feed them to the chickens."

"But I want biscuit and honey," Mae pouted, eyeing the heaped plate. "Yes'erday, she..." She pointed at Susanna. "*She* gave me a honey biscuit. It was yum."

"Shh," Naomi said to her little sister. "Remember your manners, Mae."

"I can make more," Anna offered.

"Nonsense." Samuel scooped up Mae and raised her high in the air, coaxing a giggle out of her. "We'll cut off the burned parts and eat the other half, won't we?"

Anna took a deep breath and shook her head. She was mortified. What would Mam think, if she found out that she'd served guests burned biscuits they'd picked up off the floor? Pride might be a sin, but Mam had high standards for her kitchen. And so did she, for that matter. "Really, Samuel," she protested. "I'd rather make another batch."

"Tell you what," he offered, depositing Mae on the floor and unbuttoning his coat. "I came here to offer you a deal. Maybe we can make biscuits part of it."

"I...I l-l-like b-biscuits," Lori Ann said shyly. "A-a-and I'm hungry."

"He made us egg," Mae supplied, tugging on Anna's apron. "Don't like runny egg." Anna noticed that she was wearing the too-large *kapp* that she and Susanna had put on her yesterday, while her sisters wore wool scarves over their hair. Mae's *kapp* was a little worse for wear, but it gave Anna a warm feeling that Samuel had thought to put it on her today.

"Hush, girls," Samuel said. It was his turn to flush red. "They don't think much of my cooking. Naomi's learning, but she's only nine."

"Naomi's eggs is yuck," Mae agreed.

Naomi stuck her tongue out at her sister.

"We don't criticize each other's work, and *you* shouldn't make ugly faces," Anna corrected. Then she blushed again. What right did she have to admonish Samuel's children? That would be Mam's task, once she and Samuel were husband and wife. But it was clear that someone needed to take a hand in their raising. Men didn't understand little girls, or kitchens for that matter.

"Listen to Anna," Samuel said with a grin. "It's cold outside, Naomi. Your Grossmama used to tell me that if I stuck my tongue out at my sisters my face might freeze. You don't want your face to freeze like that, do you?"

Susanna giggled. "That would be silly."

"And we're not outside."

Samuel gave Naomi a reproving look.

"Sorry, Mae." Embarrassed, Naomi looked down at her boots. Puddles of water were forming on the floor around them.

"For goodness' sakes, take off your coats," Anna urged, motioning with her hands. "It's warm in the kitchen, and you'll all overheat."

"I'm afraid we tracked up your clean floor with our wet boots," Samuel said.

Anna shrugged. "Not to worry. You can leave them near the door with ours." She motioned to Susanna. "Get everyone's coats and hang them behind the stove to dry. I have bacon ready, and I'll make French toast. We'll all have breakfast together."

"What—what about b-b-b-biscuits?" Lori Ann asked.

"Let me give you a hot breakfast, and I promise I'll make a big pan later," Anna offered.

Lori Ann sighed and nodded.

Samuel looked at his daughters shrugging off their wet coats, then back at Anna. "We didn't come to make more work for you. We ate. We don't have to eat again."

Anna waved them to the table. "Feeding friends is never work, and growing children are never full." She opened the refrigerator and scanned the shelves, choosing applesauce, cold sweet potatoes and the remainder of the ham they'd had for supper the night before. "Susanna, would you set some extra plates and then put some cocoa and milk on to heat?"

"I—I—I l-l-like c-c-cocoa," Lori Ann stuttered. Lori Ann had pale blue eyes and lighter hair than either of her sisters. Anna thought that she resembled the twin boys, Rudy and Peter, while Mae looked like her late mother.

Mae, in her stocking feet, scrambled up on the bench. "Me, too! I wike cocoa."

"If you're sure it's not too much trouble," Samuel said, but his eyes were on the ham and bacon, and he was already pulling out the big chair at the head of the table.

Anna felt better as she bustled around the kitchen and whipped up a hearty breakfast. She liked feeding people, and she liked making them comfortable in Mam's house. When she was busy, it was easier to forget that Samuel was here and Mam wasn't.

"I want honey biscuit," Mae chirped. When no one responded, she repeated it in *Deitsch,* the German dialect many Amish used in their homes.

"Be still," Naomi cautioned. "You're getting French toast or nothing."

"She speaks both *Deitsch* and English well for her age," Anna said, flipping thick slices of egg-battered toast in the frying pan.

"Louise has done well with her. I know many children don't speak English until they go to school, but I think it's best they speak *Deitsch* and English from babies on."

"*Ya,*" Susanna agreed, taking a seat between two of the girls. "English and *Deitsch.*"

"Mam says the same thing." Anna brought cups of cocoa to the table for everyone. "She says young ones learn faster. I suppose we use more English than most folks."

"She's smart, your mother," Samuel answered. "The best teacher we've ever had. The whole community says so."

Anna smiled as she checked on the browning slices of fragrant French toast. This was good, Samuel complimenting Mam. Maybe Anna hadn't ruined Mam's chances with him, after all.

"This is a real treat for us." Samuel sat back in Dat's chair and sipped his cocoa. "The neighbors, and your mother especially, have been good about sending food over, but I can't depend on the kindness of my friends forever."

Anna brought the heaping plate of French toast to the table to add to the other plates of food and sat down. Everyone joined hands for a moment of silent prayer, and then the silence was filled with the sounds of clinking silverware and eating. Conversation was sparse until the six of them finished, and then Samuel cleared his throat. "Anna—"

"Oh!" Anna popped out of her chair. "Coffee. I forgot. Let me get you a cup of coffee."

Samuel smiled and shook his head. "The hot cocoa is fine. But I wanted to ask you about that trade I mentioned."

Anna tucked her hands under her apron and looked at him expectantly.

"Gingerbread c-c-cookies," Lori Ann supplied.

"Yesterday, the kids got it in their heads that they wanted cookies. I thought we could do a deal. You make cookies with my girls, and I'll paint the bedroom. I'd be getting the better end of the deal," he added. "With breakfast *and* cookies."

"Dat brought ginger and spices," Naomi supplied. "They're in my coat pocket."

"We were out of flour and just about out of sugar. I can't get the hang of shopping for staples." He shook his head. "No matter how often I go to Byler's store, I always come home without something we need."

"Like baking powder," Naomi chimed in. "We don't have that either."

Anna chuckled. "Well, lucky for us Mam has three cans. When you go home, remind me, and you can take one with you."

"C-c-can we make—make c-c-c-cookies?" Lori Ann asked, her mouth full of French toast.

"Of course, I'll be glad to make cookies with you," Anna said, "but I can't let you paint the bedroom, Samuel. That's my job, and—"

"Ne." Samuel raised a broad hand. "It's settled. You'll be doing me a real favor. What with the bad weather and being stuck in the house, my ears are ringing from the chatter these three make. Having you bake with them will be a treat for them and a nice change for me. Besides…" He grinned as he used the corner of a napkin to wipe the syrup off Lori Ann's chin. "Maybe I'll even get to take some cookies home for the twins."

Anna sighed, gracefully giving up the battle. "If you insist, Samuel. I have to admit, I much prefer baking to painting, and I won't have to climb back up on a ladder to do it."

"Nobody's getting back on *that* ladder until I've had a chance to repair it," he said. "I brought another one in the back of the buggy." He rose from the table and rubbed his stomach. "Great breakfast. Best I've had in months."

What a good man he is, Anna thought, as she

watched Samuel put on his coat to go outside for the ladder. *And he's a good father.* Mam would be lucky to have him for a husband. Any woman would. Having him here at the table, enjoying a meal together like a family, had been wonderful, but she had to remember who Samuel was and who she was.

"Potty," Mae said loudly. "I haf' to go potty. Now!"

"Susanna, could you take her?" Anna asked. "And if you two would wash your hands and help me clear away the breakfast dishes, I'll get Mam's recipe book."

"I can read the ingredients," Naomi offered. "I like to read."

"What we need to do is find aprons just the right size for Lori Ann and Mae," Anna mused.

Now that Samuel had left the kitchen, she felt more at ease with the girls. She and Samuel's daughters would bake cookies, biscuits and maybe even a few pies. And while the oven was hot, she could pop a couple of chickens in the back to roast for the noonday meal. It would take hours for Samuel to finish the bedroom walls, and all that work would make him hungry again. She began to calculate what would go best with the chicken, and how to keep the little ones amused while she taught Naomi the trick to making good buttermilk biscuits.

As Samuel crossed the porch, he could hear

Anna talking to his girls. She had an easy way with them, and Naomi liked her, he could tell. It wasn't fair that Naomi had had to take on so many household chores since her mother had passed. If Anna agreed to marry him, Naomi could be a child again for a few years.

Maybe he'd been selfish, waiting so long to look for a wife again. He knew there were plenty who would have taken him up on an offer, but it was important that his new partner be able to love his children and teach them. It would take a special woman to fill that role, and he couldn't think of a better one than Anna Yoder, even if she was shy about giving him an answer.

He went down the steps, into the icy yard. They'd gotten off on the wrong foot yesterday, but despite the burned biscuits, today seemed different. Sitting at the table with Anna, seeing how kind she was to Mae, Lori Ann and Naomi, he wanted to court her all that much more. He was glad he'd worked up the nerve to come this morning.

Even though Anna hadn't said anything about the courting, she hadn't shut the door in his face. That was a good sign, wasn't it? Maybe she wanted more time to think about it. It was a big decision, taking on him and his family.

He paused beside the buggy and closed his eyes, breathing deeply of the cold air, letting the wet snowflakes pat against his face and lodge in his beard. He knew a father had to put his children's welfare first, but the memory of the way Anna had felt when he put his arm around her made his throat tighten and his pulse race. How good she'd felt! And she'd smelled even better, all hot biscuits, honey and, oddly, a hint of apple blossom.

She had pretty hair, Anna did, and he couldn't help wondering how long it was. Those little curls around her face meant that it would be wavy, even when she brushed it out. Anna was a respectable woman, a faithful member of the church, and it would be wrong to think of her in any way that wasn't honorable. An Amish woman covered her hair in public and let it down only in the privacy of her home...for her husband to see.

He swallowed, imagining what it would be like to touch those red-gold strands of hair, to watch her brush it out at the end of the day, to have the right to be her protector and partner.

The sound of the porch door opening behind him jerked him from his reverie. "Samuel? Do you need help with the ladder?"

He chuckled, glanced back over his shoulder and shook his head. "*Ne,* Anna. It's not heavy. I can get it." He looked at the gray sky. "But I'll put it on the porch and take the horse to the barn. It's too nasty a day to leave him tied outside."

"Turn him into the empty box stall," she called. "And throw down some hay for him."

"Ya," Samuel agreed, smiling at her.

He was rewarded with a smile so sweet that he was all the more certain that he and Anna were meant to be man and wife. The only thing standing in his way was Anna.

Chapter Four

Careful not to disturb her sleeping sister, Anna crept from her bed in the gray light of early dawn, and hurriedly dressed. Sometime after midnight, Susanna had left her own bed and slipped under the blankets with Anna, complaining that she was cold. Anna thought it more likely that she was missing Mam and hadn't become accustomed to sleeping in the room over the kitchen yet. In any case, Anna hadn't the heart to turn Susanna away, and she'd spent the rest of the night trying to keep Susanna from hogging all the covers.

The house was quiet. Usually, even at this hour, Mam would be bustling around downstairs, one of Anna's sisters would be snoring and someone would be banging on Irwin's door, calling him to get up for milking. When Anna went to a window and pulled back the shade, she understood the silence that went beyond an empty house. The ground was covered with snow, and large flakes were coming down so thickly that she could barely make out the apple trees in the orchard.

Snow... Anna smiled. Delaware rarely saw snowfalls more than just dustings, but this year had been colder than normal. She wondered if Johanna would cancel school. Her oldest sister had offered to fill in for Mam while she was in Ohio, but not many parents would send their children out to walk to school on such a morning.

Anna smiled as she padded down the hall to the bathroom in her stocking feet. Although she loved her big family dearly, it was nice to have the house quiet and not have to wait to brush her teeth or to get into the shower. And it was better yet to be able to think about everything that had happened yesterday and remember all the details of Samuel's visit, without being interrupted.

Having Mam's suitor here two days running was a wonder, and although she'd enjoyed Samuel's company, Anna wasn't certain that it was quite right for him to spend so much time here with the family away. True, Susanna had been here, but Susanna wasn't what one would call a perfect chaperone, or at least not one her Aunt Martha would approve of. Anna couldn't hold back a chuckle. There wasn't much that Mam and Anna's sisters did that pleased her aunt. Aunt Martha meant well, but in Anna's opinion, she spent far too much time worrying about the proper behavior of her relatives and neighbors.

Having Samuel at the table yesterday had been very enjoyable, so enjoyable that it made her feel all warm inside. He'd been still painting at one o'clock when she called him for dinner. Despite her earlier disasters, that was one meal that Mam would have been proud of. The biscuits weren't burnt, the chicken had browned perfectly and the rest had turned out the way it was supposed to. And Samuel had given her so many compliments that she'd been almost too flustered to be a good hostess.

A quick stop at the bathroom and Anna was downstairs to build up the fire in the woodstove before going outside for morning chores. They didn't need the woodstove to heat the house anymore because they used propane heat, but Anna loved baking in it and loved the way it made the kitchen cozy on cold mornings. Flora and Jeremiah wagged their tails in greeting, and the little terrier dashed around her ankles as Anna took Dat's old barn coat off the hook and put it on.

"Come along," she called to the two dogs, as she tied a wool scarf over her head. Although she never shirked her share of what had to be done, Anna had never been fond of outside chores. Pigs and horses made her nervous, but cows were different. Cows were usually gentle, and there was something peaceful about milking. Anna had always found it a good time to pray. She had asked Mam once if it was irreverent to talk to God in a barn. Mam, in her wisdom, had said that since the baby Jesus had been born in a stable, she could see no reason why His Father in heaven would be put out.

With Irwin gone to the auction with Miriam and Charley, Tyler, from down the road, was helping her this week. The red-cheeked twelve-year-old had already fed the horses and filled their water buckets. Both Bossy, the Holstein, and Polly, the Jersey, would be calving in the spring and had about gone dry. Tyler offered to milk them off while Anna milked Buttercup, the new Guernsey. Buttercup was as sweet as her name. She'd had a late calf and still produced lots of milk.

"Good girl," Anna crooned to the fawn-and-white cow with the large brown eyes. "Nice Buttercup." She washed the cow's udder with warm soapy water that she'd carried from the house, poured a measure of feed into the trough and settled onto the milking stool. The snow falling outside, the fragrant scents of hay and silage and the warmth of the animals made the barn especially cozy today, making Anna content. As she rested her head against Buttercup's side and streams of milk poured into the shiny stainless steel bucket, Anna's heart swelled with joy as she thought of all the gifts the Lord had bestowed on her.

She had a wonderful mother and sisters, a home that she loved and the security of a faith and community that surrounded her like a giant hug. Even the grief of her father's death more than two years ago had begun to ease, so that she could remember the good times that they'd had together. They all would have wanted Dat to live to be a hundred, but it wasn't meant to be. No human could hope to understand God's ways, least of all her. What she *could* do was work each day to appreciate the bounty He had blessed her with.

Silently, Anna offered prayers for her mother's and sisters' safe return from their journeys, and for the health of Grossmama and Aunt Jezebel. As she prayed, the level of the milk rose in the pail, smelling sweet and fresh, drawing the barn cats to patiently wait for her to finish.

She asked God to heal Samuel's sorrow for the loss of his wife and give him the wisdom and patience to tend his children. Above all, she prayed for little Mae, so far from the only home and the only mother she'd ever known. She finished, as always, with the Lord's prayer and a plea that He guide her hands and footsteps through the day to help her serve her family and faith according to God's plan. She was about to murmur a devout amen, when one last prayer slipped between her lips.

"And please, God, if it seems right, could you

find someone to marry me, someone with a heart as good as Samuel's?"

"Ya?" Tyler called from a stall away. "You said something to me?" He stood up from behind Bossy. "Not much this morning from her."

"Ne," Anna replied quickly.

She pressed her lips tightly together. She hadn't meant to trouble God with her small problems, and she certainly hadn't meant for Tyler to hear. Her eyelids felt prickly and moisture clouded her eyes. She hadn't meant to be selfish this morning, but since she had uttered her deepest wish, maybe the Lord wouldn't take it amiss.

She blinked away the tears and closed her eyes. *This is Anna Yoder again, Lord. I know that I'm not slim or pretty or particularly smart,* she offered silently, *but I think I would make a good wife and mother. So if You happen to come across someone who needs a willing partner, remember me.*

"Anna?"

Jerked from her thoughts, Anna realized that Tyler was now standing beside her. At twelve, he was losing the look of a child and starting to shoot up, all long legs and arms, but he still retained the sweet, easygoing nature that he possessed since he'd been a babe.

"Sorry," Anna said. "I didn't hear—"

Tyler grinned, his blue eyes sparkling with humor. "Falling asleep on the milking stool, I'd say." He held out his pail. It wasn't even half full. "All I could get from the two of them." He set the bucket on a feed box. "I'd best be getting to school."

"You better stop by the chair shop and see if your Dat's heard anything about school. Be sure Johanna hasn't cancelled."

"That'd be nice." Tyler grinned even wider. "Then I can go sledding." He pulled thick blue mittens from his jacket pocket. "You need me tomorrow?"

"Ne," Anna replied. "Miriam, Charley and Irwin should be back today." Anna patted Buttercup, lifted her bucket away from the cow and got to her feet.

"Unless this turns into a blizzard and they're stuck in Virginia. Irwin's lucky, getting out of school all week."

"Don't worry. Mam will see that he makes up every last math problem. And you know how he *hates* homework." After a rocky start when Irwin had first come to Seven Poplars, he and Tyler had struck up a fast friendship. Anna was glad to see it. Irwin needed friends, and he couldn't pick a better pal than steady Tyler.

"I'll see to the chickens on the way out," Tyler called over his shoulder.

Anna turned Buttermilk into a shed with the others, and then started for the house with a milk pail in each hand. She was halfway across the yard and planning what to cook for breakfast, when the two dogs suddenly began to bark, and abruptly Samuel and all five of his children came around the corner of the corn crib. Anna was so surprised that she nearly dropped the milk. Samuel? Again, this morning?

She scrambled for something to say that wouldn't sound foolish, but all she could manage was, "Good morning!"

Samuel had one girl—it appeared to be Lori Ann—clinging to his back and he was pulling another on a sled. They were so bundled up against the cold that it was hard to tell the two smallest ones apart. The twins, Rudy and Peter, trudged behind him, and Naomi trailed behind them. "Good morning to you, Anna!" Samuel called cheerfully. Lori Ann echoed her father's greeting.

"You walked," Anna said, which sounded even more foolish. It was obvious that they had walked. There was no buggy in sight and Samuel was pulling the sled. They had probably taken a shortcut across the adjoining fields rather than coming by the road.

"School is closed," Naomi supplied.

"C-c-closed," chimed Lori Ann.

"I came to finish the room," Samuel explained. His wide-brimmed felt hat and his beard were covered with snow, and it seemed to Anna as if the snowflakes had gotten as large as cotton balls since she'd gone into the barn. "To give it a second coat," Samuel finished.

"Oh." Had they eaten breakfast? What could she offer them? Anna wondered. She and Susanna had planned on oatmeal and toast this morning. The thought that Samuel had caught her at less than her best again flashed through her mind. She was wearing Dat's barn coat and her hair wasn't decently covered with her *kapp*.

"You don't have to feed us this morning," Samuel said, as if reading her mind. "I fed them all before the oldest went off to school."

"But Johanna sent us home," Rudy said. "The radio said we're getting eight inches."

Peter added hopefully, "Maybe there won't be any school next week either."

Samuel's ruddy face grew a little redder. "I have a battery radio," he said. "Not for music, but so that I can hear the news and weather. I just turn it on when it appears that there might be an emergency. Something that might affect the school or the trucks that pick up my milk."

Anna nodded. *"Ya."* Mam had a radio for the same reason, but it wasn't something that Samuel needed to know. Radios weren't exactly forbidden, but they were frowned upon by the more conservative members of the church. Of course, that didn't keep some of the teenagers and young people from secretly having them and listening to "fast" music. "That makes sense."

"We brought a turkey," Naomi said. "For dinner."

Samuel shrugged. "I'm afraid it's frozen. I wasn't expecting to bring the three oldest with me today, but I don't know how long the painting will take, and—"

"Why are we standing out here?" Anna said. She'd covered the tops of the milk buckets with cheesecloth, but any moment the melting snow would be dripping into the milk. "Come into the house. And not to worry about the noon meal. You didn't have to come back to do a second coat. I could have—"

"And another reason," Samuel said, following her toward the house. "A phone call to the chair shop, from Hannah. Roman came over to tell Johanna, at the school. Your mother won't be headed home until Sunday or Monday. Their driver is waiting to see how bad this snow is before he starts for Delaware."

Anna nodded. She missed Mam, and she knew that Susanna had hoped Mam would be returning by tomorrow. But having Samuel finish the painting would be a Godsend. That would leave her free to make the rest of the house shine like a new pin.

And having Samuel all to herself again, that would be fun, too...wouldn't it? Anna shook off that small inner whisper. Samuel was a friend and a neighbor, and was soon to be Mam's suitor. He'd come to help out for her mother's sake, no other reason. And just because she'd foolishly mistaken what he'd said about courting Mam, she had no reason to spin fancies in her head.

Then the little voice in the far corner of her mind spoke again. *But you could pretend that this was your family.... What harm would that do? Just pretend for today....*

"It would be wrong," Anna said.

"What would be wrong?" Samuel asked. "It seems to me that waiting to see if the weather's going to grow worse before starting such a long drive is good sense. You wouldn't want them to go into a ditch somewhere between here and Ohio, would you?"

"Of course not," Anna protested. "I was thinking of something else, nothing important. You come in and get warm."

"We want to stay out and play in the snow," Rudy said. "Dat said we could."

"Just the boys," Samuel said. "Girls inside."

"But Dat," Naomi protested. "I want to make a snowman."

Samuel's brow furrowed. "I need you to watch over your sisters. Anna has more to do than tend to mischievous children."

"*Ne,* Samuel," Anna put in gently. "Let her enjoy the snow. Lori Ann is a big girl. She can help me bake pies, and I have Susanna to tend to Mae. We see so little snow in Kent County. Let Naomi play in it."

Naomi threw her a grateful look. "Please, Dat," she begged.

Lori Ann was beaming.

"Well, if Anna doesn't mind. But you're getting past the age of playing with boys. Best you learn to keep to a woman's work."

Anna rolled her eyes, but when she spoke, she kept her voice gentle and soothing. "Soon enough she will take on those tasks, Samuel, and joyfully, from what I can see. She's been a great help to you these past four years."

"I can see I'm outnumbered," he answered. "But I'll not have you spoil them beyond bearing. And little Mae is a handful, as Naomi can vouch for."

Mae giggled.

Anna bent and lifted the child from the sled. "Nothing to laugh at," she admonished. "You must respect your father. You're not a baby anymore. Watch Lori Ann and see how good and helpful she is."

Lori Ann's eyes widened and she nodded, pleased by the praise. *"Ya,"* she said. "You—you must mind Dat and—and not pull t-the c-c-cat's t-tail."

Anna opened her mouth in mock astonishment. "You didn't hurt kitty, did you, Mae?"

Mae clamped her lips together and shook her head.

"Did so!" Peter said. "What she needs is—"

"What she needs is to get inside out of this cold," Anna broke in. She eyed Peter, letting him know they didn't need his two cents' worth. "Come along, Lori Ann. Let's see if Susanna is awake yet."

Samuel followed after her, not certain that Anna and the girls hadn't bamboozled him into letting Naomi stay outside against his wishes. It wouldn't be easy to court Anna with five children hanging on his shirttails, but they were his life and Anna had to know they were a "package deal," as the Englishers liked to say. As much as he loved his children, he didn't want to allow them to become lazy or disrespectful. Naomi was nine, after all. He tried to remember his sisters at that age. Had they been running wild with the boys at nine?

They stepped up onto the porch and stamped their boots to knock most of the snow off. Then Anna got a broom and handed it to him. Slipping out of her galoshes, Anna carried Mae inside, leaving him to help Lori Ann.

"I—I—I l-like Anna, Dat," Lori Ann whispered in his ear as he leaned down to pull off her boots.

"I like her, too," he agreed, but he had to admit that he was somewhat troubled by what had just happened. The thought that if he married, his wife would actually have *more* influence on his children's behavior than he would crossed his mind.

It was right, of course, but he'd been used to doing things his way ever since Frieda had passed on. He supposed there would be adjustments he'd have to make, adjustments that he hadn't thought about. And Anna would have to make adjustments, as well. After all, the man was the head of the house, and Anna would have to learn to respect his wishes.

Not that she was the bossy type. Not his sweet, sweet Anna. Even now, when she'd gone against him, it had been asking, not telling. He wouldn't let her spoil them, for certain, but he wanted to be a reasonable man. He didn't want to give Anna the wrong impression that he was like her Uncle Reuben, who hopped every time his wife, Martha, said jump. But neither did he want to scare Anna off. After all, he was a lot older than she was—sixteen years, give or take some months. It wouldn't do for her to think he would be a stern and unyielding husband.

Susanna held the door wide. "Come in," she called in her high, singsong voice.

Anna's little sister was smiling, as always, and Samuel smiled back. Of all of Hannah's girls, Susanna was the easiest. In some ways she was as wise as an old woman, and in other ways as innocent as Lori Ann. But no matter which Susanna greeted them, she always made him feel good inside.

"I'm going to get right to that painting," he said to Anna, "but if these two give you a minute's problem, you call me or Naomi to deal with them."

"*Ya,* Samuel, I will," Anna said softly.

He set the frozen turkey in the sink, removed his outer garments and hung his gloves behind the stove to dry. "Sorry the bird isn't thawed. Roman brought it from the freezer at the chair shop. I didn't think about how long it would take to—"

"I'll manage," Anna assured him. "Leave it to me."

Samuel started right in on the second coat, and by the time Anna called him for dinner, he had finished three quarters of the room and his stomach felt as if he hadn't eaten for days. As he came into the kitchen, he walked into a wave of delicious smells: cinnamon, hot bread, chicken and dumplings, apple pie and more.

All of his children were already seated at the table, faces shining clean, hair slicked back and cheeks as red as cranberries. "No turkey," Peter informed him.

"Chicken and dumplings," Rudy said. "Turkey tomorrow."

"Not that I expect you to come back tomorrow," Anna hastened to say. "But I'll set it to roast tonight, and by morning it will be done. If you send the boys to fetch it, you can—"

Samuel felt his face grow warm. "I'll be back

tomorrow," he confessed. "Rather, some of us will. That bedroom floor and the hall need a fresh coat of that dark red. I've got a few gallons left from when I painted my place, and I was planning on—"

"I can't let you do all this work here," Anna said. "You must have chores at home."

"Not so many. Not this time of year, and I've got the two hired boys to keep busy. I'll be back to finish up tomorrow, unless you…" He hesitated, not knowing what more to say, not willing to hear her say she didn't want him here.

"Ya," Susanna pronounced. "Make nice for Mam and Grossmama and Aunty Jezebel."

Anna put a huge bowl of mashed potatoes in the center of the table. "I don't know what to say," she protested.

Susanna beamed. "Say thank you."

"Th-thank you," Anna repeated.

"Good. That's settled," Samuel said, taking Peter's hand for grace. "Now, I'm starving. Let's get to this good food before it gets cold."

Dinner was every bit as good as the previous day's. He was a man who liked his food and Anna was one of the best cooks he'd ever known. Eating like this every day would be one of the real pleasures of having her as his wife. Not that he was marrying her for her housekeeping or her cooking skills, but a kitchen was the heart of the house, like a wife was the heart of the family.

By late afternoon, Samuel had finished painting the walls and gathered his brood for the walk home. The snow had tapered off, and there was not quite eight inches, but a good six, and it was so cold that it wouldn't melt anytime soon. Playing in the snow had tired his three oldest, and it seemed that Anna had kept the two little ones occupied in the kitchen all day. They were going home almost as heavily laden as they'd come, with a gallon of vegetable soup, biscuits and cinnamon buns for supper.

The following day, the three oldest stayed home to do chores and play in the snow, leaving Samuel with just the two youngest girls to carry along to Anna's house. To his relief, Anna and Susanna seemed just as pleased to see him, Lori Ann and Mae as they had before. And the house smelled of roasted turkey, just as Anna had promised. "I don't want to impose on you," he said as they entered. "It's just that it's a lot to leave them with Naomi when she has work to do."

"Nonsense," Anna said. "You know we love to have them. Lori Ann was a big help with the cinnamon buns yesterday. And today she can help me with raisin pies."

Lori Ann nodded excitedly.

"Mae's a little cranky," Samuel said. "I think she needs to go back to bed. She had nightmares again last night, and she was awake for hours."

"Not to worry," Anna assured him as she gathered Mae in her arms. "Susanna will make her feel better."

"Don't want a nap," Mae grumbled.

Samuel quickly escaped to his painting, leaving Anna to handle Mae. Getting his youngest adjusted was harder than he'd expected it to be. He loved her dearly, but it was hard to *like* the child when she whined and fussed half the time. And when she dissolved in tears, crying for his sister Louise, he felt completely helpless. It was so much easier to leave her to Anna and Susanna.

About an hour into his work on the floor, Anna came in with a steaming cup of coffee and a cinnamon bun.

He smiled at her and took a sip of the coffee. It was strong, just the way he liked it. "You're a wonder, Anna Yoder," he said.

She stood for a moment, tall, her cheeks rosy, twisting her hands in her apron. "Samuel, I don't know what..." She trailed off, then looked up at him through thick lashes. Anna's eyes were beautiful, wide and brown and sparkling with life.

She looked vulnerable, so sweet that he wanted to gather her in his arms as he'd seen her do with his little daughter. He wanted to taste her lips, to smell her hair. He wanted to claim Anna as his wife before God and his church.

Wanting her so badly gave him courage. "Have you thought any more about what I said before, about courting—"

"Courting Mam," she said, answering so quickly that he didn't get to finish.

"What?" He blinked, unsure what to say. Surely, she didn't think…

She nibbled at her lower lip. "Mam. You said you want to court Mam. Before… Didn't you?"

"Hannah?" His face flamed. "*Ne.* Not Hannah. What would give you that idea?"

"But you said—"

"It's *you* I want to court, Anna Yoder," he said in a rush. "Not your mother. Not any other woman in Kent County. Just you."

Chapter Five

Anna's eyes widened as she backed up to lean against the freshly painted wall of the bedroom. "Oh." She felt as though she might faint. "Oh, my. I…I misunderstood. I was sure you said…but then…" She paused to catch her breath. "I thought I was mistaken…about what I heard."

"You were, if you thought I said it was Hannah I'd come to court." Samuel balanced the paintbrush carefully on the edge of the can, and came to stand in front of her. "Anna, I didn't mean to give anyone the wrong idea…but…it's been you all along I've been interested in."

She couldn't wrap her mind around what he'd said, yet there was no doubt what he'd meant. *Samuel Mast had said that he wanted to court her.* Was she awake or asleep and dreaming?

"Anna." He reached out to take her hand and she drew it back and shook her head.

"Give me a moment," she said. First she hadn't been able to catch her breath, now she felt like she was breathing too fast. "It's…it's a surprise."

Samuel folded his arms across his broad chest. The expression in his eyes grew serious and she saw his Adam's apple constrict. "A good surprise or a bad one?"

"I'm not sure." She felt silly with him standing here towering over her, but she felt so addled that if she stood up she might faint—not that she ever had before. Samuel reached for her hand again and childishly, she tucked it behind her and shook her head. If he touched her, she knew she'd lose all ability to think clearly. "Why me?"

"Why not you, Anna? I'm older than you, that's true, but you're of legal age."

"But all this time…I thought…everyone thought that you and Mam were going to—" She could feel herself choking up, knew she was going to cry. She never cried, but suddenly she couldn't stop the tears from welling up in her eyes.

"Don't cry. Why are you crying? I thought you'd be happy."

Anna covered her face with her hands. He'd been so happy this morning, and now she feared she'd angered him.

"I like your mother," he persisted. "I admire her, but I've been thinking about you for a long time. I think we would make a good match."

Samuel was saying words she wanted to believe, but her heart told her they weren't possible. She was what she was—the third daughter of a widow...the Plain Yoder girl...the *sturdy* girl. How could Samuel Mast choose her? He was handsome. He had a fine farm, and he was a solid member of the community, a deacon in the church. Any family would be proud to have him marry one of their daughters or sisters. He could pick and choose from all of the unmarried girls and young widows of Kent County, or any other Old Order Amish settlement in the country. Why would he pick her?

"But, your wife..." she stammered. "Your Frieda was beautiful."

"*Ya.* She was. But she's gone, Anna, and I'm alone. Too long, I think. The children...sometimes they're more than I can manage."

She looked up at him, barely able to string four words together. "I see why you need a wife. Everyone in Seven Poplars sees. But why me, Samuel?"

His face reddened. "We are both hard workers. You're a good cook, a good housekeeper." He cleared his throat. "And...and a faithful member of our church. I think you would make me a fine wife."

"I see." *Good cook. Good housekeeper.* Honest words, so why did they cut into her like sharp thorns? Had she expected Samuel to declare his love for her?

"Tomorrow is church," he said stiffly. "I want to…" He swallowed again. "Can I come for you and Susanna to drive you to service?"

"Ne." She shook her head. If they arrived in Samuel's buggy, everyone would notice. There would be talk. *"Ne,* Samuel," she repeated, recovering some of her composure. "Not for everyone to see. You must give me a few days to think and pray about this. Church is at Roman and Fanny's. Not far for us to walk."

He looked hurt. "You don't want to go to church with me?"

She wanted to squeeze his hand, to reassure him, but she was afraid to touch him. She couldn't trust herself. "Best if we keep this idea between us for a while," she said. "To be sure it's what we both want."

He took a deep breath and the lines around his eyes crinkled. *"Ya.* I can see that might be wise," he said, "if you are not certain." Disappointment puckered his mouth. "But not too long."

So that he can choose someone else if I refuse him, she thought. "Marriage is a big step," Anna said, feeling better, but still not completely herself. "I need to talk with my mother."

Samuel looked at the floor, then at her again. "So you will speak to Hannah about my proposal?"

Anna nodded. "Who knows me better than Mam?" She tried to smile, but was unable to cover her nervousness. "You have to try to understand. My doubts are not of you, Samuel, but of myself." Her mouth felt dry. "It's just that it is so sudden."

He nodded. "So you have said." He turned, as if to return to his painting, but then stopped and turned back to her. "It's not my age, is it? I'm not a raw boy, but—"

"Anna! Anna!" Susanna shouted from the hall. "Come quick. Miriam and Charley! And Irwin!"

Jeremiah began to bark, and Anna heard the sound of voices in the kitchen. "Smells like roast turkey," Irwin said.

Anna looked at Samuel meaningfully. "Just between us?"

He frowned and nodded. "Go and greet your sister and her husband," he said. "I will finish this."

With a sigh of relief, Anna hurried from the room. With Miriam and Charley back, the house would echo with good talk and laughter. They would be full of news of the auction and the people they'd seen. She would think about Samuel's request for permission to court her later. She would have time to think and to decide what was best for her and for him. She would need to pray harder than she ever had before.

If she said yes to Samuel, her whole life would change in more ways than she could imagine. She would leave her home to go to his…to be his partner and helpmate—to mother his *five* young children. It would be hard, but she would do it willingly, if only she knew for certain that he wanted her for the right reason. But the fear that he didn't pressed hard on her heart.

Marriage was forever. The Englishers might separate or divorce, but never the Plain folk. If she said yes, she would be bound to Samuel and to his will so long as they both drew breath.

Again, his words echoed in her head. *"You are a hardworker."*

What he was saying was that theirs wouldn't be a love marriage like Miriam and Charley's, or like Ruth and Eli's. What if Samuel would be marrying her for her strong back and skill in the kitchen? Again, she thought of Johanna, her relationship with her stern husband, and the tears her sister shed when she thought no one was looking.

Anna didn't know if she could exist in a marriage like that. It would be like settling for half a loaf when she wanted the whole, hot and fragrant from the oven—when she wanted it so bad she could taste the sweet goodness of the bread on her tongue.

"Anna!" Her twin sister, Miriam, shook the snow off her coat, dropped it onto a kitchen chair and threw open her arms. "I've missed you," she cried.

"And me?" Susanna demanded. Samuel's two

youngest clung to her hands, giggling. "You missed me, too?"

"Ya," Miriam agreed, hugging first Anna and then Susanna. "The auction was fun, and I saw lots of cousins and friends. But Charley and I were ready to come home yesterday. We couldn't find a driver who was willing to head out late in the day, not with the weather."

"And we bought three horses," Irwin said excitedly. He had Jeremiah in his arms, and the little terrier was licking his face. "One is for me. Charley bought a horse for me."

Anna looked to Miriam. "A horse? Charley bought Irwin his own horse?"

"More colt than horse," Charley supplied. "He's a two-year-old, and he needs work, but if Irwin is willing to work with him, he'll come around and make a good driver." He grinned. "Is that turkey I smell? We left early and didn't stop for lunch on the road."

"Plenty for all of us," Anna assured him. "Samuel brought the turkey. He's been helping out by painting, getting the bedroom ready for Grossmama and Aunt Jezebel."

Miriam's brows went up. "Samuel? Samuel's been here painting?"

"Ya," Susanna said. "Anna broke the ladder and spilled the paint."

"Shhh," Anna said. "Remember what I told you."

Susanna nodded. "You said not to tell about—"

"Later," Miriam said, interrupting Susanna's tale. "I think these men are hungry. We should get dinner on the table and share our news later."

"Amen to that," Charley agreed. "I could eat a whole turkey, feathers and feet."

"You usually do," Miriam teased. Smiling, she shooed Susanna and the little girls toward the china cabinet. "Set the table," she said.

Anna mouthed a silent *thanks* to her twin. Another second, and Susanna would have spilled the beans. The last thing she wanted was for Charley and Irwin to hear that Samuel wanted to court her. Irwin was as bad as Susanna for telling things a person didn't want told. She supposed little brothers were like that, and although Irwin wasn't really kin, since he'd come to live with them he'd begun to feel more and more like he was one of them.

But what was there for anyone to tell? Samuel had asked to court her, but she hadn't agreed, and she wasn't ready to share her secret yet—not even with Miriam.

The following day, Anna sat in the midst of her three sisters, closed her eyes and let the peace and beauty of the familiar hymn enfold her. Not everyone in the community had made it to services, due to the icy roads, but Roman and Fanny's small house was still packed to the walls with worshipers. Ruth and Eli had returned from their travels. Now only Mam and Grossmama, Aunt Jezebel and her youngest sisters, Leah and Rebecca, were absent.

Although, had the whole family been here, Anna didn't know where they would have found room to sit. The congregation was certainly growing, and that was a blessing. But if the church grew too large they would have to split, and Anna couldn't imagine not seeing Samuel and his children, all of her sisters, the Beachys, or all of their closest friends at services every other Sunday.

Bishop Atlee was offering the sermon this morning with the assistance of Preacher Uri Schwartz, visiting from Tennessee. Preacher Uri told about the Good Samaritan and used the story to elaborate on the importance of getting along with the Englishers while maintaining a distance from the outer world.

Anna shifted on the bench and tried not to look in Samuel's direction. Lori Ann had started off sitting with Susanna, but had tired of playing with her handkerchief dolly and had wiggled through the row of men to sit on her father's lap. Mae was in the kitchen with Johanna and another young mother, and Naomi was seated between Susanna and Miriam. Samuel's twins, always a handful, sat directly in front of him, so that he could keep an eye on their mischief.

As much as she wanted to concentrate on Preacher Schwartz's sermon, Anna's thoughts kept drifting back to Samuel and their conversation the previous day. She'd slept only fitfully last night, for thinking about him. What was she to do? She wanted to accept his proposal; it was a dream come true to most girls. But was it just that? Something not real? A dream…or a mistake on Samuel's part? Whatever reason had caused him to seek her out, Samuel would soon come to his senses and see that it was a bad choice. That he could do better.

There must be a half-dozen other young women he could choose from in Kent County alone, all of them more attractive than she was. Sitting in the row behind her were Mary Byler and Amy Troyer, both unmarried and of courting age. Either of them would be suitable, and either would be thrilled to have Samuel propose to them. And they were both pretty.

It was all well and good for Mam to say that "true beauty comes from inside," because her mother was beautiful. Her mother loved her, Anna knew that, but Hannah Yoder had never looked out at the world from Anna's eyes.

The congregation rose for a hymn and Anna stood with them. As she opened her book, she glanced at Samuel, only to find his gaze on her. Her breath caught in her throat, and she felt tingles run from her fingertips to her toes. Immediately, she averted her eyes and stared down at the Old German text, but moisture clouded her vision and a single tear drop fell onto the page.

Lord, help me, she prayed silently. *Help me to be strong, to consider Samuel's proposal with both my head and my heart.*

Susanna's off-key voice rose beside her and Anna reached over and squeezed her hand. Obviously, God hadn't meant for Ruth to remain home with Mam and Susanna, as Ruth had once believed. But maybe God meant for Anna to sacrifice having a family of her own to help her mother. She could be happy, living with her mother and her little sister, and tending to Grossmama and Aunt Jezebel, as well. She didn't need a husband and children of her own to fulfill her life, did she? Not all women were given the gift of children; her sisters would give her nieces and nephews to love and care for.

A final prayer ended the service. Men and boys began to file outside while the women flowed toward the kitchen to prepare to serve the communal meal. This was one of the best things about church Sundays. Anna loved making and serving good food to those she loved. She felt most at ease in the kitchen, and it never failed to make her feel useful to see that others were well fed.

"Anna," her cousin Dorcas called. "Come down to the cellar with me and help fetch up the macaroni salads. Fanny ran out of room in the kitchen for all the food."

Anna nodded and followed Dorcas through the narrow door off the hall and down the steep steps. The basement was dim. The only light present was the weak winter sunlight filtering through several windows at ground level. Downstairs, Roman had fashioned a spacious storage area for Fanny to place her rows of home-canned tomatoes, green beans, sauerkraut and corn. Naturally cool but unlikely to freeze, this area was perfect for keeping baskets of potatoes, sweet potatoes, apples and pears through the winter months.

A long table covered with newspaper held pies, cakes and four giant bowls of macaroni salad, potato salad, three-bean salad and pasta salad. "Do you think we'll have enough to eat?" Anna teased.

"I sure hope so," Dorcas said, going along with the joke. "My father can eat all of this and ask for seconds."

"*Ya,* he does like to eat," Anna agreed, "but my question is, where does it all go?" Uncle Reuben was a stringbean, tall and lanky. No matter how much he ate, he never seemed to gain a pound.

Dorcas giggled and used a plastic fork to scoop up a bite of the potato salad. "Johanna's," she pronounced. "I like the way she makes her dressing."

Anna nodded. "She's a good cook, my big sister."

Dorcas captured another bite. "Umm. Can you

manage more than one bowl, or should we make two trips?"

Anna hesitated. She'd promised Samuel she wouldn't say anything to anyone but Mam, but her secret was rubbing like a blister on her heel. Her mother hadn't gotten home yet, and if she didn't share her problem with someone, Anna thought she would burst. "Can I tell you something?" she said impulsively.

Dorcas shrugged. "You tell me stuff all the time."

Anna put a finger to her lips. "This is different. A secret…"

Dorcas giggled. "You've decided to turn English and buy a motorcycle like Eli used to have?"

"*Ne.* Be serious. I need to ask you something important."

Dorcas picked up the bowl of four-bean salad and studied it. "Lydia's, I think," she said. "She puts too much vinegar in her sauce." Then she realized that Anna was watching her intently and shrugged. "So what is this big secret?"

"Samuel Mast asked if he could court me," Anna blurted. There, it was out. She'd said it, and the house hadn't fallen in around them, and the stars hadn't fallen from the heavens. She felt better already.

"Mmm-hmm," Dorcas agreed. "Sure he did." She chuckled. "You wish."

"*Ne.* True. Yesterday. Well, actually, before that, but—"

"Your mother's beau suddenly decided he wants you instead?" Dorcas grimaced. "Bad joke, Anna."

Anna shook her head. "Not meant to be funny. He asked me. At first I thought that he was asking about Mam...you know, if I minded. But that wasn't it. He told me he never intended to ask Mam to marry him. He says he wants to marry *me,* Dorcas."

"Not possible."

"That's what I thought, but he means it."

"And your mother? What will she think—that you stole her beau while she was in Ohio fetching your grossmama?"

"No, you don't understand. We were mistaken. Mam and me. All of us. Samuel said he thinks of Mam as a friend, but that it's me he wants."

Dorcas pursed her lips. "You think maybe he asked her and she said *ne?*"

Anna swallowed. "It's possible, I suppose, but I think Mam would have told me—told us. He didn't say anything about asking her. I don't think he did." She hesitated. Dorcas was sampling another salad. "So what do you think?"

"I think it's a better match than you could hope for. Samuel's nice, and he's got a big farm. But are you willing to take on five stepchildren?" She pointed with the plastic fork. "That won't be easy. And that youngest is a handful."

"I think I could, with God's help. I really do. They are such sweet children, especially Lori Ann."

Dorcas rolled her eyes. "And the twins? Rudy and Peter? *Sweet?*"

Anna shrugged. "They're eleven-year-old boys. Full of themselves."

"*Ya.* Those two are. Tried to burn down the school, didn't they? Not to mention your barn."

"Not on purpose," Anna said. "Samuel's done a good job, but the children really need a woman—a mother—in the house."

"Maybe." Dorcas hesitated, swallowing another mouthful. "Are you sure, Anna? Are you sure you're not mistaken, not wishing so hard for someone that you've…"

"Made all this up?" Anna felt hurt. "It's true. Samuel asked me if he could court me. I wouldn't tell you if it wasn't. I thought you would be happy for me."

"I *am* happy for you." Dorcas shrugged. "I just wouldn't want you to be mistaken."

"I'm not mistaken," Anna said firmly. "And Samuel wants an answer, but I don't know what to say."

"Do you like him?"

"'Course I do. Who doesn't like Samuel?" But she didn't tell the entire truth about how he made her feel. Not even to Dorcas could she admit that she more than liked him. She couldn't explain how just watching Samuel made her heartbeat quicken or how the sound of his voice made her feel like she'd bitten into a ripe Golden Delicious apple. "It's just…I don't know why he would pick me," she finished in a rush.

Dorcas nodded. "You know I love you, Anna. It doesn't matter to me if you're…you know."

"Fat?"

"Sturdy," Dorcas supplied, "But you know you aren't one of the cute girls. Neither am I. So you have to wonder if he asked you because your mother owns the farm next door or maybe because you cook so good."

The backs of Anna's eyes prickled. What Dorcas was saying was no more than what she'd thought herself, but it still hurt hearing it out loud. "He's looking for a housekeeper and someone to watch his children," she murmured.

"Maybe he loved his Frieda so much that he doesn't want to feel that way about a second wife." Dorcas's mouth turned up in a crooked smile that showed her broken tooth. "What you have to decide is if it matters. If having Samuel as your husband is more important than marrying someone who adores you—like Eli does your sister Ruth. Not everybody can have that."

Anna sighed and she nibbled at her lower lip.

"I didn't mean to hurt your feelings." Dorcas put down the fork. "You asked me, and I—"

"*Ne.* You didn't hurt my feelings," Anna said. "I wanted the truth, and I knew you'd tell me exactly what you thought. It's what I thought, too, that maybe he was thinking more of the house and his kids than what *he* wanted."

"I'd take him anyway," her cousin said. "Having a husband like Samuel any way at all, has to be better than being an old maid."

"Maybe so," she agreed. It would be an answer to her prayers, wouldn't it? Having Samuel to cook and sew for…maybe, if the Lord was willing, maybe having babies with him.

"It would be enough for me," Dorcas whispered, reaching for one of the big bowls of salad. "So you grab him and hold onto him if you can. Because if he looked in my direction, I'd take him up on the offer in an Englisher's minute."

Chapter Six

Outside, in Roman's long, open carriage shed, the men of the congregation gathered. It was a time to relax after the long and thought-provoking sermon. Neighbors shook hands, exchanged news about the various families' health, talked about the weather and what they would plant in the spring, and waited for the women to call them to the communal meal.

Samuel and Charley were discussing the merits of the new stock Charley had purchased at the Virginia auction. Samuel was keeping a sharp eye on Rudy and Peter when Shupp Troyer sauntered up and stuck out his hand.

"Awful cold for January, ain't it?" Shupp grabbed Samuel's hand and pumped it.

Samuel nodded. "This is when we generally get a warm spell before February hits." He was still watching his twins, who, for once, seemed to be on their best behavior. The boys were standing with Lori Ann amid a crowd of children at Roman's back porch, where Anna and Miriam were handing out apples, buttered biscuits and small meat pies that would tide the little ones over until they got a chance to come to the table.

Samuel could remember how hungry he used to get, waiting for the elders and guests, all the men and older boys, and finally the women and babies to eat before it got to the children's sitting. As usual, Anna Yoder had remembered the children and their growing appetites. He felt a surge of pride that she had such a good heart. He knew that if she accepted him, she'd make a good mother.

"Weatherman calling for more snow tomorrow." Shupp droned on as he scratched his chin. "Don't usually get snow when the temperature drops this low. Makes it hard to tend to the animals. And makes my sprung back ache like a toothache."

Not that you do much tending of anything around the farm, Samuel thought. He'd never seen Noodle Shupp Troyer work a full day since he'd come to Delaware, and that was before his two daughters married and brought strong sons-in-law into his house to pick up the slack. Noodle could always be depended on to have some ailment to complain about at any gathering. Luckily for him, his girls had taken after his wife, Zipporah, and were as industrious as honey bees.

"Heard you was doing some work for Hannah," Noodle said slyly. "Been traipsing up there a lot this past week, ain't you?" He raised one side of his bushy eyebrow. Noodle had a single eyebrow that extended in a thick line from the far corner of his left eye, over his nose, to the corner of his right eye. It was so wooly that Samuel once took it for a knit cap under the man's hat. "Guess there was need, with Hannah still away."

"I did some painting for the Yoders," Samuel admitted. "What with Jonas's mother coming to stay." He was an easygoing man, and this was the Sabbath. It wouldn't do for him to let Noodle's gossiping ways get under his skin or cause him to have uncharitable thoughts.

"Some of Hannah's girls home to watch the farm, ain't they? That big one, Anna?" Noodle chuckled and elbowed Samuel. "Now, she'll make an armful for some man."

Samuel gritted his teeth and forced his voice to a neutral tone. "Anna's a good girl," he said. "And there's no better cook in the county, for all her being but twenty-one. You've no call to poke fun at her."

Noodle tugged at his eyebrow, pulling loose a few gray hairs and dropping them into the straw underfoot. "No offense, but sayin' that she's hefty ain't no more than the honest truth. 'Course…" He grinned at Charley. "Once Samuel here makes the widow his wife, it's natural he'll be scramblin' to find that one a husband—seein' as how she'll be his stepdaughter."

Charley's normally genial expression darkened. "Anna may be bigger than most girls, but her heart's big to match."

"Never meant no..."

The clang of Fanny's iron dinner triangle signaled the first seating. As a deacon of the church, Samuel was one of those so honored, and for once, he didn't mind leaving Charley and the younger men to join Reuben and Bishop Atlee and the others. If he stayed here any longer with Noodle Troyer, he'd say or do something that wouldn't set a good example for the younger people on a Church Sunday. He was a peaceful man, but he had his limits.

Noodle wasn't the brightest onion in the basket, and Samuel doubted he meant any harm, but he was slighting Anna with his loose talk. He had to knot his fists to keep from tossing the man into the nearest horse trough.

Lots of people would be sticking their noses in when he and Anna started officially courting, but that was their shortcoming. Anna and he were right for each other. Her size wasn't a problem for him, and it shouldn't be anyone else's concern. He thought she was perfect, in a homey and comfortable way that a wife ought to be, and she had the most beautiful eyes. He was glad that Charley had stuck up for Anna, and he wished he'd said more. But it wouldn't be right to tell Noodle or anyone else what he figured on doing, not until he and Anna settled things between them.

As he crossed the snow-covered yard toward the house, he looked up and caught Anna watching him from the back step. Her basket, once full of foodstuffs, was empty, and the children had scattered to eat their prizes, but Anna still stood there, tall and fine in her starched *kapp* and best Sunday dress. It made him go all warm inside at the thought that she was watching him.

He smiled at her, but she didn't smile back. Her eyes went wide like a startled doe, and she darted back inside and slammed the door. Instantly, the good feeling in his chest became a cold hollow.

What if Anna didn't care for him in that way? What if she thought of him only as a neighbor and a fellow church member? What if he'd laid his heart open and she wouldn't have him? What then?

It was after three, when everyone had eaten and the young men were packing the benches into the church wagon, but Samuel still hadn't had a minute alone with Anna. She'd stayed in the kitchen, instead of serving at the tables, as she usually did. Now, when he had all five of his children gathered up and waiting in the buggy, he went to find her.

Fannie met him at the back door, and Samuel could see the kitchen was still crowded with chattering women cleaning up the last of the dishes and stowing leftover food. "Could I speak to Anna?" he asked.

"Anna Yoder?" Mischief sparkled in Fannie's eyes.

What Anna did she think he meant? The only other one he knew that was here today was three years old. "*Ya,* Anna Yoder."

All the women in the kitchen were staring at him through the open kitchen door, and he felt his face grow hot. Growing up with older sisters, he'd always felt that women were so different from men that they might have been a different breed altogether. They always seemed to have secrets; and put two women together, and no matter how much he liked them, a man always felt tongue-tied.

Like the other day, when Anna had asked why he wanted to marry her, his brain had frozen and he'd mumbled something about hard work, when that hadn't been what he wanted to say at all. He *did* admire Anna for her cooking and her skill at sewing and such, but he would have wanted her if she couldn't boil water or thread a needle. It was her quiet way he loved most, her gentle nature and her generous heart. Any man ought to be able to see that Anna shone like wheat in a basket of chaff, and should be honored to have her walk out with him. But saying those fancy love words out loud were more than he could manage.

"Samuel?"

He blinked. He'd been daydreaming and not seen Anna until she was standing right in front of him. Susanna was right behind her; her little round face peered around Anna, full of curiosity.

"Like to take the two of you home," he managed. "Maybe more snow. Sun be going down soon…get your feet wet." His stomach knotted and he broke out in a cold sweat beneath his heavy coat. What was wrong with him, that he couldn't speak to Anna easy-like, as he had a thousand times since she was a young girl?

"Going with Charley and Miriam." Susanna peeked around her sister. "In Charley's buggy."

"Our things are already loaded," Anna said. "They're coming to Mam's for coffee and evening prayer."

"Ah. So you won't need a ride?" His heart sank. He'd hoped to drive her home, maybe go in for coffee and visiting.

"*Ne.* It's thoughtful of you to ask." She smiled and closed the door while he stood there, leaving him feeling both disappointed and a little hurt.

He tried not to let any of his emotions show as he made his way to his buggy, but when he went to climb up in the front seat, his mouth dropped open in astonishment. Sitting there was not his little Mae or Naomi or even Lori Ann. Martha Coblentz was planted solidly on the bench, her feet against the kick board, her mouth tight and her shoulders stiff beneath her black wool cape.

"Martha?" He did a double take, wondering for a moment if he'd started to get in the wrong carriage. But, no, this was his horse, Smoky, his buggy, his five kids giggling in the back. *What was Martha doing here?* "Is there a problem?" he stammered. "Is your horse lame?"

"'Course not," Martha said. "Don't talk foolishness, Samuel. I've been wanting to have a good talk with you for a long time, but you're a hard man to catch up with." She waved her hand. "Well, don't just stand there. Get in."

"Am I driving you to your house?"

She shook her head. "Reuben will be along to bring me home. Drive on to your farm, Samuel. You're blocking Lydia and Norman in."

With a sigh, Samuel did as he was told. No good could come of this. He didn't need to be a smart man to know that. Martha, sister to Hannah Yoder's dead husband, and Reuben's wife, was full of advice, and he was certain he was about to receive a good measure of it, whether he wanted it or not.

"I feel it's my duty to talk sense into you," Martha said as they crossed the blacktop road in front of the chair shop. "You know that Frieda and I were close."

Not that close, Samuel thought, but he held his tongue. Frieda had once confided to him that she thought Martha should keep her nose in her own affairs, but... He stifled a groan. Frieda would have also been the first one to caution him about uncharitable thoughts on the Sabbath.

"She was a good wife, a good mother, a faithful member of the church," Martha intoned. "Your Frieda was one of the best. You'll not find her equal."

Samuel nodded and kept his eyes on the horse's rump. The road was icy, so he didn't want to drive fast and take a chance on the animal slipping. "She was and is still dear to me and the children."

"But she's gone on to a better place," Martha continued. "Frieda's with God. And you're here. With five children to raise. A house and a farm to run. You have responsibilities, Samuel, big responsibilities."

He nodded again. Did she think he didn't know that? That he didn't pray for guidance every day—that he didn't worry about his children? That he wasn't lonely for a woman's smile and soft word?

"It's common knowledge that you've been calling at Hannah's regularly for the past two years," Martha said, turning to look at him over her spectacles.

Samuel passed the lines from one hand to the other. The wind was blowing full into their faces, and he felt sorry for the horse. Luckily, they didn't have far to go, just past the schoolhouse to his lane, and that had trees on either side, to shield them from the icy blast. "Hannah's lost her husband," he said, "and she's been a good neighbor. It would be less than my duty to neglect her."

"I'd say nothing bad about Hannah," Martha went on. "Wasn't she my own dear brother's wife? But you're a young man, still in your prime. You've a big farm, and you need more sons to help in the fields. Hannah's too old for you, Samuel. There. I've said it to your face."

"Hannah's hardly over the hill."

"She's a grandmother. And too old to give you more children. You need a young woman, and I know of one who's secretly had affection for you for a long time."

Suddenly understanding why Martha had approached him, Samuel straightened in the seat and began to smile. Relief eased the hard knot in his chest, and he didn't feel the cold anymore. Martha hadn't come to lecture him. She'd come as a go-between for Anna, her niece.

"You understand, I never intended to court Hannah," he admitted. "We're friends, nothing more."

"That's good to hear." Martha didn't sound entirely convinced.

Smoky turned into the lane so fast that the

buggy skidded sideways. The girls shrieked and Martha clutched the edge of the seat. Samuel reined the animal to a walk. "You'll be in the barn soon enough," he soothed. Roman's place was close, no more than half a mile. Had it been just him and the two boys, they would have walked over to church, but it was too bitter a day for his daughters.

"My, but that gives a body a start," Martha said, still clutching the seat. "We could have turned over."

In the back of the buggy, the squeals had turned to giggles and whispering. Samuel decided the best course was to ignore them.

"*Ne.* We were in no danger. Just the lane's slippery." More snowflakes were beginning to float down, large, lacy ones that reminded him of meringue on one of Anna's lemon pies. The sky was already dark in the east, and the air smelled of snow. They might get a few more inches before it was done. He decided to keep the cows inside tonight. "It eases my mind, you telling me this," he admitted. "I was wondering whether she was favorable toward me or not."

"Oh, she favors you well enough, but she's modest, as an unmarried girl should be. But she thinks of you a lot, enough to make a chicken pot pie for your supper tonight. I tucked it into the back of the buggy, wrapped in toweling to keep it warm. Along with some potato salad and apple cake. You'll not have to do a thing. I'll put the food on the table and Naomi and the girls can set out the dishes and flatware while you're doing your chores."

The house came in sight, and behind it the barns and sheds that housed his animals, wagons and machinery, all quickly becoming frosted in white snowflakes. As it was the Sabbath, no work was permitted by the *Ordnung,* but the chickens and ducks, the pigs, the horses and cows still had to be fed and watered, and there was still a night milking to do.

"It's thoughtful of you and of her."

"It's the least I can do, seeing how much I loved your poor Frieda. You've been a widower too long, Samuel. People have been wondering why you haven't remarried. It's your duty to your children and to your community. There always seem to be more available girls than prospective husbands."

"I thought maybe I was too old for her—that she'd want a younger man, someone closer to her own age."

"Then you're wrong. The best marriages are those where the man is older and more settled in his ways. You can guide her both spiritually and in her daily responsibilities. Young husbands are flighty, by my way of thinking. A proper husband needs to be the authority in the house."

A small smile came to Samuel as he pondered who was the authority in the Coblentz house. He guided Smoky around to the back of the house. "Help your sisters out," he ordered the boys.

"Oh, it's snow—snowing," Lori Anne cried.

"Snow," Mae echoed.

"Take the little ones inside," Samuel said to Naomi. "The door's unlocked. And keep Mae away from the stove." As the children hurried toward the house, Samuel turned to face Martha. "I want you to know that Anna and I were properly chaperoned when I was there painting. I'd do nothing to cast suspicion on her name or mine. Susanna and my children were with us all the time."

"I'm glad to hear it. Rumors are easier to prevent than to erase, once they've begun. It behooves a man in your position to always be above criticism."

He climbed down and helped Martha out of the buggy. Peter came to take hold of Smoky. "Unharness him and turn him into his stall," Samuel said. "Then change your clothes before starting the chores." He glanced around, half expecting to see Reuben's carriage. "You did say that Reuben was coming for you, didn't you?" he asked Martha.

"I wasn't sure how long our talk would take. He'll be along. I'll just make a pot of coffee and see to it that the girls are doing their evening chores. They need guidance as much as boys, you know. They've been too long without a mother's direction."

"I suppose," Samuel agreed. He took Martha's arm as they went up the steps to the open porch. "You can take off your boots inside," he said. There was a utility room just inside, with benches to sit on and hooks for winter coats and hats. "Just make yourself to home."

Inside, the house was warm, and Lori Ann's tiger cat was pleased to see them. Purring, it curled around Martha's ankle as she pulled off first one wet boot and then the other. "Reuben doesn't hold with animals in the house," she said. "Hair and dirt. Animals belong outside."

"I'm afraid I spoil my children," he admitted. "And the cat's a good mouser." He pointed to a pair of Frieda's old slippers on the shelf. "You can put those on. Warmer on your feet than just stockings." He excused himself to go and change into his barn clothes. Having Martha in the house felt a little awkward. He knew what a snoop she was, but she'd come to bring him the great news today, and he would never treat her unkindly. "Coffee's over the stove," he called over his shoulder.

As he padded down the hall in his stocking feet, he could hear Martha giving sharp orders to his girls. There was a basket of laundry on the floor near the table, left there since yesterday. He wished he'd folded and put away those clothes last night. Martha would be sure to notice that and the breakfast dishes still standing in the sink. She was right, he supposed. He did need a helpmate. Soon he'd be ready for unexpected company anytime.

When he returned to the kitchen, he found the coffee pot simmering and his two older girls busy setting the table for a light supper before the children went to bed. Mae was under the table hugging the cat, and her eyes were red, as if she'd been crying. "What's wrong?" he asked, holding his arms out to her.

"She's wet her drawers," Martha fussed. "A big girl like her, nearly four. She should know better. I told her to just sit a while in them and see how it felt."

Samuel frowned. He'd changed his share of diapers and wet underthings since Frieda died. Martha might know best. Such was usually women's business, but it didn't seem right to him, to punish a little girl for an accident. "She's still not settled in here yet," he defended. "Accidents are bound to happen. Naomi, could you take your sister and see that she's dressed in dry clothing?"

Naomi nodded. "Come on, Mae," she said, extending a hand. Sniffing, the little one crawled out, took hold of her sister and shuffled after her, out of the kitchen. Lori Ann stopped, mouth open, a plate in her hand and stared longingly at her sisters.

"What? You want to go with them?" Samuel asked. She nodded, and he took the plate and motioned her away. "Go on, then."

Martha took down two mugs and set them on the counter with a loud thump. "You make their new mother's task no easier," she said. "Spare the rod and spoil the child. My Dorcas will have her hands full."

It was Samuel's turn to stare, gape-mouthed. "Dorcas? What has Dorcas to do with anything?"

Martha cleared her throat. "You're not usually so thick. Who do you think I've been talking about all the way from Roman's? My daughter, Dorcas, the girl you'll soon be walking out with."

"Dorcas?" He shook his head. "But I didn't..." He dropped into a chair, suddenly feeling as if his head might burst. "There's some misunderstanding, Martha. I never intended to court your Dorcas."

"Nonsense. Who else would you choose? She's unwed, nearly twenty-five, and has been brought up to know her duty." She made a sound of disbelief. "Sometimes I think men are blind. Of course, Dorcas. She's exactly right for you, and now that I've brought it to your attention, Reuben and I will expect you to begin making formal calls on her within the week."

Rudy banged open the kitchen door. "Reuben's here, Dat. He says for Martha to hurry. Snow's getting worse, and he wants to get home before dark."

"I didn't intend to court Dorcas," Samuel repeated. Was it possible that he'd completely mis-understood? That it was Dorcas that Martha had come to speak for and not Anna? "Dorcas made the chicken pot pie for me?"

"I said so, didn't I?" Martha snapped. "Honestly, Samuel, I don't know what to think about you. You always seemed so sharp-witted to me, not a man that had to be hit over the head with a thing before he saw the right of it." She followed Rudy out into the utility room, plopped down on a bench, and began to pull on her left boot as his son vanished through the outer door.

Samuel caught a whiff of something unpleasant, and Rudy's quick exit set off a warning alarm in his head. "Don't—" he began.

Martha jammed her foot into the boot and let out a scream. She leaped to her feet and began to hop on her right foot, yanking at the left boot. "What have they done?" she shrieked as she stared at her filthy black stocking and the unmistakable smell of wet cow manure permeated the room. "Monsters!" she accused. "Your sons are monsters!"

Chapter Seven

The following day, at four in the afternoon, Anna's mother, grandmother, great aunt and two younger sisters arrived in the hired van. Instantly, the house, which had been relatively quiet with only Anna, Miriam, Ruth and Susanna in the kitchen, rang with laughter and eager chatter. There was a great deal of hugging, stamping of snowy boots, exchanging of news, talk of the snowy roads and thankfulness that the long winter trip had been completed without mishap.

"We saw a terrible accident near Harrisburg," Leah said as she squeezed Susanna for the third time. "A bus overturned."

"There were police and ambulances," Rebecca added. "But our driver spoke to one of the firemen who was directing traffic. He said that he didn't think anyone was killed. We prayed for them."

Aunt Jezebel nodded. Anna hadn't seen her

Grossmama's younger sister in years, but she didn't look a day older than the last time she'd visited Delaware, and she certainly didn't appear to be a woman in her sixties. She was small and neat with an Ohio-style *kapp,* a rose dress with long sleeves and cape, black stockings and black lace-up, leather shoes. Aunt Jezebel's glasses were thin silver wire rims, which often slid down to perch on the tip of her small nose; and her hair, once red like Anna and her sisters', had faded to mousy-brown with silver streaks.

According to Mam, Aunt Jezebel wore only rose-colored dresses, never any other color, even on Church Sundays. She was shy and only spoke amid close family, and then as quiet as a mouse's squeak. Anna didn't believe that Aunt Jezebel was touched, as some people whispered, no matter how odd some of her habits were.

Johanna had once confided that Aunt Jezebel had been courted by a boy from Lancaster when she was seventeen. Her parents had felt that Jezebel was too young to marry and had refused to agree to the match until her next birthday. She had waited patiently, but on the day of her wedding, her bridegroom never arrived and no one ever saw him again. What happened to him was a mystery; some people thought he'd run away to become English, others suspected something worse had befallen him. Regardless, Jezebel never recovered from the shock, and had remained single all these years. Anna thought it all very tragic and romantic.

Now, amid the noisy welcome, Aunt Jezebel perched on a chair in the corner of the room like a small rose-colored sparrow. She watched Grossmama, Mam, and Anna and her sisters with bright blue eyes, waiting for someone to tell her what to do next. Aunt Jezebel would do anything you asked of her, and she was a tireless worker, but she never seemed capable of deciding what needed to be done on her own. Usually, it was Grossmama who gave the orders, and Aunt Jezebel carried them out with quiet efficiency.

"It's cold in here." Grossmama, a tall, imposing woman with big hands and a stern countenance, made a great show of sniffing loudly. "I knew that we should have waited for spring. I took a chill in the van and my neck hurts. The driver put on her brakes so hard when we stopped at that Englisher food-fast for lunch that I twisted it." She rubbed her back and glared at Mam. "You should have packed more sandwiches. That chicken was tough—and expensive. Three dollars for a little dry chicken on bread. Ridiculous." She rapped her cane on the floor. "Jezebel. Find my shawl."

"Here it is, Grossmama," Leah said, draping a black wool shawl around the old woman's bony shoulders.

Grossmama picked at the weave of the shawl.

"Not this one. It itches. Jezebel! Where's my gray shawl?"

Behind Hannah's back, Rebecca grimaced and rolled her eyes for Anna's benefit. *It's starting already,* Anna thought. Their grandmother was nothing, if not consistent. Nothing ever pleased her, least of all their mother.

"I'll fetch it, sister," Aunt Jezebel said obediently. She hurried across the room to sort through a large, old-fashioned zippered bag. "Here." Removing the offending black shawl, Aunt Jezebel placed another around her sister's shoulders, a wrap that appeared to Anna to be identical to the first, other than its color. Aunt Jezebel folded the black shawl neatly and tucked it into the bag, carrying the satchel back to her chair and standing it by her feet before taking her seat again.

"My stomach isn't right," Grossmama proclaimed. "Is there any clear broth?" She peered at the clean white tablecloth, as if hoping to find a stain.

"I made chicken soup," Anna said. "I remembered that soup was always easy on your stomach when you were unwell. It's on the back of the stove. Shall I dip some out for you?"

"Chicken soup? Does it have noodles?"

Anna nodded. "Egg noodles."

"Are they store-bought? Store noodles give you worms. They have bugs in them. I never eat store noodles." She turned her gaze on Susanna. "The Englishers put bugs in them."

"*Ne.*" Susanna shook her head. "Anna rolled the noodles. I cut them." She beamed.

Grossmama nodded. "Well, at least someone is thinking of my health." She patted Susanna's chubby hand. "*Danke,* Susanna. You should've come to Ohio, instead of those two." She waved a hand at Leah and Rebecca. "Silly as hens, both of them. Fancy girls. Trying to act English. Take after you, Hannah."

"Now, Lovina," Hannah soothed. "I'm sure that Rebecca and Leah did their best to help you." Mam never called Grossmama mother, always by her name. Grossmama had insisted on it years ago, when Mam had wed Dat. She'd said pointedly that Mam was not a daughter, but a daughter-in-law, and that she shouldn't be pretending blood kinship where there wasn't any.

"Hmmp," Grossmama grunted. "That one." She indicated Leah with a bob of her chin. "She's not Plain. She draws boys like flies to honey. Comes of you giving her such an outlandish name—an Englisher name."

"You're tired," Hannah said, ignoring the last remarks.

Anna knew that there was no sense in Mam pointing out to Grossmama that "Leah" was from the Bible, and that it wasn't her fault that she'd been born beautiful. It was true; everyone noticed how pretty Leah was, and boys especially noticed. Leah's picnic baskets had always been the first one auctioned off at community fundraisers, and had usually brought in the most money.

Secretly, Anna had wondered if her sister had gotten both of their shares of looks. Not that she was jealous of Leah. She wasn't. Leah was her sister, and she loved her. God had made Leah as she was, as God had made her, and their grandmother was wrong to accuse Leah of trying to be English because she had a pretty face. Dat always said that Grossmama was hard on Leah because she'd been a notoriously Plain child and a Plain woman. It had been the Lord's will that Anna take after Dat's side of the family and not Mam's.

"And I want those little crackers, the ones with no salt," Grossmama said. "Salt will kill you."

Anna looked at Rebecca, who shrugged. "Water crackers, I think," her sister said. "We bought them from the big supermarket in town…in Ohio. I've never seen them here."

"I should never have come," Grossmama whined. "Jezey, didn't I tell you we should never have come? I don't like Delaware. I never have. I'm going home tomorrow."

"She needs…she needs her rest, I think," Aunt Jezebel whispered to Anna. "Such a long trip is hard on her, and her arthritis pains her."

"Exactly right," said Mam, who had excellent hearing. She glanced at Ruth. "If you and Miriam could get her into bed, I'll have Susanna bring her the chicken noodle soup and some of those sweet white peaches we canned last August."

Grossmama headed toward the back door and Ruth took her shoulders, gently turning her in the right direction. "This way to the bedrooms, Grossmama."

"I know which way," Grossmama insisted. "And I don't want chicken soup. Bring me toast with honey. And herb tea. Blackberry. And some meat. Scrapple. I don't suppose you have any decent scrapple. Jonas likes it crispy with ketchup. You never could get the recipe right, Hannah. You were hopeless when it came to scrapple. Jonas always says so." She narrowed her eyes and looked around. "Where is he? Why isn't he here?"

Mam sighed. "Jonas is in the barn, Lovina. Milking the cows."

"Ne," Susanna said. "Dat's not in the barn. He's—"

"In God's hands, as always," Mam interrupted. "You'll see him later." She gestured to Ruth and Miriam, and they led Grossmama out of the kitchen and down the hall toward the newly painted bedroom.

Anna could hear Grossmama fussing. "Jonas

likes his scrapple just so. The way I make it. Hannah…"

"But Dat isn't milking the cows," Susanna protested. "He's in…in—"

"He's in heaven," Anna said. "But Grossmama forgets."

Susanna looked puzzled.

"Dat was her son," Mam explained. "And your grossmama is old. It's all right if she pretends that your father is alive. You don't want her to be sad, do you, Susanna?"

"Ne."

"Sometimes she remembers," Aunt Jezebel whispered. "And then Lovina cries and cries." She got to her feet to follow the others to the bedroom and nearly tripped over Grossmama's bag. She gave a little yip, turned around three times, sat down and got up again. Anna knew that was one of Aunt Jezebel's odd habits, and everyone but Susanna pretended not to notice as she hurried out of the kitchen after her older sister.

Anna glanced at Rebecca, who just shrugged. It was simply Aunt Jezebel's way, and they'd all have to get used to it.

Hannah hugged Anna and Susanna again. "I've missed you all terribly. How is everything? Did the school have to close for snow?"

"Just the one day," Anna answered. "Has Grossmama been like that for the whole trip?"

Hannah chuckled. "Worse. But it must be difficult for her, having to leave her home, not knowing if she'll ever return. And your grossmama has many aches and pains. You must all do your best to welcome her and make her feel wanted."

Mam accepted a mug of coffee from Susanna and settled into a chair at the table. "I've had enough traveling for a while. I can tell you that. And I was gone less than a week. I don't know how Leah and Rebecca managed for so long without being homesick."

"We were," Leah said, coming to sit beside her mother. "We missed all of you terribly."

"Me too?" Susanna asked.

"You most of all," Leah assured her.

"You're lucky you got that one home," Rebecca teased, indicating her sister. "There were four boys who wanted to marry her."

Leah smiled, making her beautiful face as rosy as an angel. "Not four boys," she corrected. "Two boys and two men."

"One was fifty," Rebecca confided. "Can you believe it? He had a long, scraggly beard and he chewed tobacco." She wrinkled her nose. "Yuck."

"I'm not getting married for years and years," Leah said. "I've missed you all too much. And I wouldn't want to be so far away. When I marry, I'll pick someone from Kent County, so we can still come for Anna's dinners."

Four suitors, Anna mused. And Leah wouldn't be twenty-one for two months. "I cooked enough for a crowd," she said to her mother. "I imagine Johanna will be over with the children as soon as she hears—"

Irwin opened the kitchen door and Jeremiah ran in. The little dog barked and ran in circles before darting under the table. "Company," Irwin announced. He grabbed a biscuit off the tray on the gas stove and left the kitchen so fast that he didn't stop to take off his heavy denim jacket.

"Johanna?" Mam asked. Her question was answered as Aunt Martha and Dorcas appeared in the doorway. "Come in." Mam rose to her feet. "It's good to see you."

"My duty." Martha shed her coat and the scarf she wore over her *kapp.* "What with Mother arriving." She handed the coat to Dorcas. "Do something with this."

"Ruth and Miriam are getting her into bed," Hannah said. "We fixed up the room across from mine for her and Aunt Jezebel. You can go in and see her if you like."

Aunt Martha turned her scorching gaze on Leah. "You're not wearing paint, are you? Your cheeks look awfully red."

Rebecca smiled. "No, Aunt Martha. Leah's cheeks are red from the cold. And it's good to see both of you, too."

"Hmmph." Aunt Martha looked pointedly at the coffee pot.

Anna caught the strong scent of bleach. Aunt Martha always smelled of bleach; and when she was small, Anna had wondered if she bathed in it every night. She hurried to pour her aunt and Dorcas a cup. "Two sugars, Aunt Martha?" she asked. "And milk?"

"Cream. I always use cream. It's good for my stomach condition."

"No cream or sugar for me," Dorcas said. "Just the coffee."

"Thin as you are, a little sugar and cream would do you good," Aunt Martha said as she took Dat's seat at the head of the table. "I'll give Mother a chance to get into bed. Too much excitement isn't good for a woman her age."

"I hope Reuben is well," Hannah said.

"Toothache. Been bothering him all week. He's in the carriage. No sense in him coming in. We're not staying," Aunt Martha said in her piercing nasal voice. "Just doing my duty as a daughter. Mother and I will have lots of time to visit, and I don't want to tire her on her first day home."

"Maybe I should—" Anna began.

"*Ne.* You stay right where you are. It's only fair that you hear what I have to say. I don't like to drop this on you when you've hardly caught your breath, Hannah. But you have a right to know."

Mam sighed. "*Ya,* Martha. What is it I should know? Miriam hasn't been riding motor scooters again, has she?"

Susanna's eyes grew huge. "Miriam has a scooter?"

Aunt Martha sat up to her full height and tightened her thin mouth. "Samuel Mast has been making noises about wanting to court your Anna. It's ridiculous, of course. You need to put a stop to it before Anna gets her heart broken or becomes a joke."

"Anna?" Rebecca asked incredulously, turning her gaze on her sister. "But I thought Samuel and Mam were…were…"

Anna felt her face flush.

Martha turned around in her chair to address Rebecca. "Am I talking to you, girl? I'm talking to your mother, and it would behoove you to hold your tongue and show some respect."

Anna's stomach turned over as she gripped the back of one of the kitchen chairs. She opened her mouth to protest, but no sound came out. She glanced at her mother to see Mam's questioning look, and felt her face grow even hotter. She'd had no chance to speak to Mam, yet; she hadn't expected Aunt Martha to bring the news so quickly. She never should have talked to Dorcas before talking to Mam.

"I don't know what's gotten into the man. Has

he buckwheat for brains? Probably his frustration with his poorly behaved children. They're out of control, I tell you."

"Ne." Anna bristled. "Samuel's children—"

"I'll not have you defend them. They are monsters," Aunt Martha declared. "Those twins put fresh, runny cow manure in my boots last night. Can you believe it? Ruined a pair of perfectly good boots. I'll never get the stink out of them. Samuel's buying me a new pair. You can be certain of that. But don't tell me that the lot of them are better than wild little animals."

"Cow manure?" Susanna echoed.

Leah coughed, put a hand over her mouth, and fled the kitchen. Rebecca and Dorcas were hot on her heels.

Cowards, Anna thought. She looked back at Mam. She wasn't smiling.

"If they did that, they certainly deserve punishing," Mam said. "I'm sorry about your boots, but what does that have to do with Anna and Samuel?"

"Dorcas tells me he wants to court Anna. Samuel's gone soft in the head, I tell you. I told Reuben to speak to the bishop. You know Samuel can do better than Anna."

"And how could he *do better than Anna?*" Mam asked. Her voice was low, her eyes cool.

Anna knew that look, and knew that this was no place for Susanna. Quickly, Anna moved to the stove, dipped a bowl of chicken noodle soup, added a spoon and pushed it into her little sister's hands. "Take this to Grossmama," she ordered.

"But she wants crackers," Susanna said.

"Soup first," Anna said, and Susanna did as she was asked.

"Why is that so strange, that Samuel should want to take my Anna to wife?" Mam asked, folding her arms over her chest and taking a step toward Aunt Martha. "What is wrong with Anna?"

Anna's chest felt tight. Tears stung the backs of her eyelids. She was ashamed, and she didn't know why. She wanted to run after her sisters, but she wouldn't leave her mother to face Aunt Martha's sharp tongue alone. If she didn't have the nerve to defend herself, she would at least stand with Mam.

Aunt Martha's face turned the color of lard and her mouth pursed. "Not wrong, maybe," she said. "Just not...not proper."

"How not proper?" Mam persisted. "My Anna is a good girl." Mam now glared at Aunt Martha with a gaze hot enough to fry eggs. "Why wouldn't Samuel want her?"

"Well, because she's..."

"I'm Plain, that's what she means," Anna whispered. She felt sick. "Too Plain for a man like Samuel Mast." She blinked and sat down hard.

Unbidden, a bad memory came back to her, a memory that haunted her dreams. She'd been in second grade, maybe third, but she was chunky then, the fattest girl in the school.

Someone had left a big section of pipe on the edge of the schoolyard. The boys started crawling through it at recess, and one day, Miriam did, too. Then, all the smaller girls wiggled through the pipe.

Anna refused to join them until the King boys started teasing her, shouting, "Fat, fat, the barn rat."

"She is not!" Miriam had protested. "You can do it, Anna. Show them!"

Against her better judgment, Anna had tried to crawl down the dark pipe, but at the end, where it got even smaller, she'd gotten stuck. She started to cry, and the teacher came running to see what was wrong. The only way they got her out was when Ruth crawled down the pipe and pulled her backwards by her feet.

In the process, Anna had torn her *kapp* and her stockings, and all the kids laughed. She was so upset that she'd thrown up all over her new blue sneakers in front of everyone.

"You see," Aunt Martha flung back, ripping Anna out of her thoughts. "Anna sees it. She knows she's fat. You're blind, Hannah, blind to the faults of your girls."

"And how, exactly, is it Anna's fault if God has made her beautiful in a different way?"

"Not only her size…her looks. It's not…not appropriate," Aunt Martha stammered. "What with Samuel courting you for so long. People will talk."

Mam closed in on Aunt Martha. "Who says that Samuel was courting me?"

"Why…why, everyone. Everyone knows he was. Now, suddenly, it's Anna he wants. It might likely be Leah next week. Or Rebecca! It's not right. Not fitting."

"No matter what you think, no matter what *anyone* thinks, there was never an understanding between me and Samuel. He is my good friend, Martha. Nothing more. And if he wishes to court Anna, or Leah for that matter, both girls are of age to walk out with a decent man of our faith. And, who they choose to be with is none of your affair."

Aunt Martha grabbed her coat and threw it around her shoulders. "Dorcas!" she shouted. "Dorcas! We're leaving."

"You are always welcome in my home, sister," Mam said. "But only if you can refrain from insulting one of my girls."

"I came here out of the goodness of my heart," Aunt Martha flung back. "So that Anna wouldn't be shamed in front of the community."

"I thought you came to see your mother and Aunt Jezebel."

"That, too. Don't change the subject. You're too bullheaded to listen to common sense, Hannah.

You always were." She planted both feet and settled her hands on her bony hips. "There are more appropriate choices for Samuel Mast, and he will soon come to realize that. He will never marry your Anna, no matter what you think."

"Anna," Mam said gently. "Would you show your aunt out?"

Anna swung open the door to the porch and a blast of icy air struck her full in the face. She gasped. Samuel was standing on the porch, his fist raised to knock. "Samuel?"

"Anna." He took a step forward onto the threshold and stopped, half in the kitchen and half out. "I came to speak to Hannah…and to you."

"Samuel." Martha sniffed. "I should think you would have a great deal to say for yourself—for your actions."

Anna turned to meet her mother's gaze.

"Come in, Samuel," Hannah said. "Martha was just leaving."

Samuel looked from Mam to Aunt Martha to her. "Anna, if I could talk to your mother… Say what I should have said…"

"Take my word on it," Aunt Martha pronounced. "You'll be sorry you didn't ask Dorcas. She'll not be available long!"

"Mother!" Dorcas, her face as red as a radish, cried. "Don't—"

"I'm the one voice of reason," Aunt Martha

said. "You'll all come to see that." She pushed past Samuel and out of the house. Dorcas seized her coat and ran after her, looking as if she was about to burst into tears.

"Have I come at a bad time?" Samuel asked.

"Ne," Anna said, taking down Dat's big brown mug and pouring him a cup of coffee with shaking hands. "I think you have come at *exactly* the right time."

Chapter Eight

Samuel stood there, frozen to the spot, until Hannah nodded. "Sit down, Samuel," she said, sitting down. "We do have much to talk about."

He sat at the table, holding his coffee mug between his big hands and wishing he were anywhere but here. "The last thing I wanted to do was make trouble for you, Hannah, or for your family."

Mam motioned toward the coffeepot, and Anna took her mother's cup and refilled it. Anna carried the steaming cup to Hannah and joined them at the table. "Mam…" she began.

Hannah shook her head. "I think we should let our guest tell us why he's come. It's a cold afternoon, with evening chore time coming on fast. It must be important, to bring Samuel here."

"Ya," he agreed. "It is. But maybe you and me should talk, Hannah. Alone?" He glanced at Anna. She looked as if she had been crying, and he felt

a stab in his gut. He'd never wanted to hurt Anna. But there were Hannah's feelings to consider, as well. Had he given the impression that he was courting her? If he had, he'd betrayed their friendship. And it wouldn't be right for him to begin courting Anna without settling the matter.

"My Anna is a grown woman and dear to me," Hannah replied. "Whatever you have to say, you may say to both of us."

He nodded. "All right." Stalling for time, he took a sip of the coffee. Somehow he swallowed wrong, coughed, and then choked, spitting coffee across the table and feeling like a total dumbkin. "Sorry," he blurted. "I didn't mean—"

Anna silenced him with a smile. "There is no need. It's easily fixed." She went to the sink, returned with a cloth and wiped the tabletop clean.

"Now, what has my sister-in-law in such a stew?" Hannah asked. Her expression was serious, but a hint of amusement lurked in her eyes.

Anna turned her gaze on her mother. "It's a long story, but while you were gone, Samuel came to paint and—"

"Never mind the painting," he said. "That's not important. I'm afraid I've…I've hurt your feelings, Hannah. Did you think I've been courting you these past two years? If I caused you to—"

Hannah held up a palm. "Hush, Samuel. What

I might have wondered and what I was certain of are two different things. You never asked, and I never did either. You're too good a friend to me and to my daughters to let a silly misunderstanding come between us. The truth is, if you'd outright asked to court me, I would have refused. In my heart, I'm still Jonas's wife. Maybe my love for him will always come first, but I know that as much as I care for you, it was never in that way. You're a good neighbor, and we've shared laughter and tears together, but nothing more."

"So you're not angry with me for wanting to court Anna?"

"Ah." Hannah steepled her hands, and Anna made a soft sound in her throat. "So it *is* true? You two are walking out together? Without consulting me? Without asking my permission?"

Samuel rose to his feet, knotting his hands nervously. "I wanted to speak with you. I meant to, but…" He glanced at Anna, trying to figure what she was thinking, and then looked back at her mother. "You're right. I should have asked you." He exhaled. "None of my reasons seem all that good, now that I think on them."

"Sit down," Hannah said gently. "Drink your coffee. The worst is over. Now we can talk, friend to friend, *ya?*"

He still wasn't sure if he was welcome here. "Anna?" he said. "Do you want me to leave?"

She shook her head. "*Ne,* Samuel," she murmured.

She looked small and helpless, and he wanted to wrap his arms around her and hold her so tight that he could feel the beat of her heart, but he knew that was out of the question. Hannah might still refuse her permission, and then what would they do? Anna would never go against her family for him, would she? He wished he hadn't come. He wished that he'd waited until he could talk to Anna again, to see how she felt.

"Widowers with children often marry girls younger than them," Hannah said. "Clary and Moses Peachy? He had seven children."

"But Clary was in her thirties, with a child of her own," he said, taking his seat again.

Hannah studied her daughter for what seemed like centuries, but he knew it could have been only a few seconds. His chest felt so tight that he thought he would explode.

He cleared his throat. "Hannah, I ask your permission to court your daughter, Anna," he said woodenly. "In every way that is proper and according to our custom. And if we suit each other, I want to make her my wife and the mother to my children."

Hannah pursed her lips. "Was that so hard? Samuel, Samuel, you men make things more difficult for yourselves." She cut her eyes at her daughter, who was blushing. "Now, you must ask Anna if she wishes you to court her."

"He did," Anna managed in a small, breathy voice. "I told him that I wanted to talk with you first and pray on it. Then I made the mistake of confiding in Dorcas. She must have told her mother last night after church, after Aunt Martha stopped by to see Samuel." She looked at him. "I'm sorry, Samuel. I should have known Dorcas would tell her mother."

Hannah reached across and patted Anna's hand. "Who knew what or when they knew it isn't all that important. My question is, did you give him an answer? Do you want him to walk out with you or not?"

A lump rose in Samuel's throat. This was exactly why he had been putting off asking Anna. Because this was it…or could be. Right here at this kitchen table Anna could say she had no feelings for him, that she never could. And that would be the end of it. There would be no more dreams of cozy evenings in his kitchen with Anna…or sharing his warm bed with her.

Anna broke through his worries with a long sigh. Moisture flooded her beautiful eyes. "I haven't had time to think it out," she said.

"Have you prayed about this, Daughter?" Hannah asked.

"*Ya,* I have, but I'm still confused."

"Is there no chance for me, then?" he asked, his voice sounding shaky in his own ears. "Is there someone else you'd rather—"

"I told you," Anna said, all in a rush. "It isn't you. You're...wonderful. It's me I'm not sure about."

She thought he was wonderful. Relief turned his bones to warm butter. "I'm not too old for you?" he ventured.

Anna shook her head. "You're exactly the right age." She looked down at her clasped hands. "The boys my age seem so...so feather-headed to me sometimes. And you're different...more sensible."

"Does the thought of being mother to Samuel's five children frighten you?" Hannah asked, taking Anna's hand again and squeezing it. "It isn't wrong to feel that way. Better that you admit it, if that's how—"

"I love his...your," she corrected. "I love your children," she admitted shyly. "Even the twins, who find trouble like Irwin finds laziness. They are good, sweet children, all of them, and I can see how they need the care of a mother."

He drew in a ragged breath and his heartbeat quickened. "Then why won't you..."

Hannah raised her hand again. "Listen to her, Samuel. I think what Anna is saying is that she needs time to decide what is best to do...time to get to know you."

"But she's known me most of her life," he protested.

"But as Samuel," Anna put in. "I've known you as our neighbor, as our deacon, and as a member of the school board—not as...as..."

"Not as a beau," Hannah finished. "She's right, Samuel. You've dropped this on her quickly. Anna's not had much experience at riding in a buggy with a young man, or sitting with him on the porch swing."

"It's a little cold for porch swings, don't you think?" he asked.

"What I mean is, my Anna is not a flighty girl. I've kept her close at home, maybe more than I should have. She's always such a help to me."

"I know she is...must be. I mean to court her properly, but how can I, if she won't agree...if she's not willing?" He stood up and went to Anna's side and looked down at her. "This has not been a decision I've made lightly. I've thought about you for a long time...prayed for guidance." He gazed into her eyes. "Anna, I believe God intends you to be my wife."

"Lots of people *think* they know what the Lord intends," Hannah said. "It may be that this is right. But there can be no harm in waiting a little longer, so that Anna can be sure."

Anna averted her eyes, but he could see that she was trembling.

"I think my Anna would be glad to have the opportunity to consider your proposal, but she doesn't want to commit herself yet. Is that right, Anna?"

She nodded shakily. "That's it exactly, Samuel. I want time."

Disappointment made his reply gruffer than he intended. "How much time were you wanting?"

Anna cast a desperate glance at her mother.

"What if we say by her next birthday?" Hannah suggested. "She will be twenty-two on the twenty-fifth of February. Would that suit you, Anna?"

Anna nodded. *"Ya."*

"And you, Samuel? Is that agreeable to you?"

"Ya," he agreed. "I've waited this long, I can wait a few weeks more. But I hope that I can call on Anna…that we can spend time together before that."

"I think that would be lovely," Hannah said. "So long as she feels comfortable. Would you like that, Daughter?"

Anna nodded again, glanced up at him, and offered a tremulous smile. "I think I would."

"It's settled then," Hannah said, bringing her hand down on the table. "And we'll keep this between ourselves until the two of you come to a firm decision. No sense in giving Martha and the other gossips more fuel for the fire."

"Hannah!" An older woman's shrill voice sounded from the back of the house. "Where's my Jonas? He can't still be milking those cows."

Hannah rose to her feet. "Anna's Grossmama. She's tired from the trip and a little confused. I should tend to her." She smiled. "Anna, would you pour Samuel some more coffee?"

He shook his head, moving around to the other side of the table. "*Ne.* Best I be heading home. See what those rascals of mine are up to. Cows will need tending soon."

"No need to run off," Hannah assured him. "Stay and have another cup. I believe I saw a pumpkin pie in the refrigerator. You're welcome to a slice."

"I should be going," he said.

"You have time for pie." Anna got up. "I made four. There's a pear pie you can carry home to the children."

His mouth watered at the thought of Anna's piecrust. He'd had a slice of Dorcas's chicken pie the night before, and the crust was soggy. Anna's were always good. And if Hannah was leaving them alone, there was something else he wanted to talk to Anna about. The bad thing about being a single father was that there wasn't anyone to share the responsibility of the children. He had to make all the decisions alone, and he was thinking that Anna might be someone he could talk to about what was worrying him. If she became his wife, he liked to think they would spend lots of time talking and making decisions together.

He nodded, and before he knew it Hannah had vanished down the hall, and Anna had slid a big wedge of pie in front of him. She went to the stove and came back with the coffeepot. "Go ahead. Dig in," she said. "I have to wait for the others for mine. After supper, I mean." She grimaced. "Not that I don't like pie. I do. You can see that I like just about everything."

He paused, a forkful of pear and flaky crust in midair. "I always liked a body with a good appetite," he said. "My Mam and my sisters. They like to eat."

She smiled shyly. "Sometimes I feel funny, eating in front of other people. They stare at my plate…you know. Like I must be a pig to be so big." She sighed. "But I was born big, Mam said, over nine pounds. And that wasn't anything I did wrong."

"Nine pounds." He washed the mouthful down with a sip of coffee. "The twins didn't weight that between them. Came out like scrawny little skinned rabbits. I was afraid they'd never live. Frieda had a time getting them to eat. Was months before they started looking like normal babies."

"But look at them now," Anna replied. "Healthy and hale, praise God. Bright boys, too." She sat down at the table, close enough for him to make out the little specks of dark brown in her light brown eyes. He sighed, thinking what a fine figure of a woman she was.

"Those boys are a handful," he admitted. "And..."

"Is there something?"

He nodded. "It's what they did to Martha."

"The cow manure in her boots?" Anna asked. The corner of her full lips twitched in amusement.

"Ya," he said. "That."

Anna clapped a hand over her mouth, but couldn't suppress a giggle, and before he could stop it, he began to laugh, too. "And she stepped in it?" Anna squeaked, before breaking into a full-bodied shriek of laughter. "Poor Aunt Martha."

He began to choke. She jumped up and slapped him on the back, and suddenly they were both roaring with laughter. Tears rolled down his cheeks as he remembered the look on Martha's face when she pulled her stockinged foot out of the boot and stared in disbelief at the manure. "And the stink!" He snorted, and they were both off in peals of laughter again.

"I wish I could have seen it," Anna said, when she'd gotten control of herself enough to speak again. "Poor Aunt Martha."

"Lord forgive us," he rasped, wiping his eyes

with the back of his hands. "It was wrong of Peter and Rudy, rude and disrespectful."

"Ya," Anna agreed. "Very disrespectful. But funny to see, I'm certain."

He burst forth with another chuckle, one so deep that it shot up from the pit of his belly. "And it's disrespectful for us to laugh at her misery. For a deacon of the church to—" And he was off again, choking with laughter.

"For which, I'm sure, we shall both ask forgiveness in our prayers," Anna said, in a properly meek tone. Her gaze locked with his, and he saw the twinkle in her eyes.

"Amen," he said, wiping his eyes again. "Oh, I haven't laughed like that in…in forever. Either you are very good for me or…"

"Very bad," she teased.

He looked at her with new respect. He'd never realized Anna Yoder had such a sense of humor about her, or the ability to bring out the child in him. There was a lot more to this bighearted girl than tasty pie and light biscuits. There was a deep well of fun and good-natured joy. "I have to punish them, of course," he said. "I can't let it go—such disrespect to an older person."

Anna nodded. "And a guest in your house. It was wrong of them."

"They take after my father, they do," he said. "Dat was always up for a good joke. Once he got up in the night and put something in his brother's cow dip, so when Uncle Harry started to run his herd through the water to kill the lice in their fleece, they turned purple. He had three purple cows before he realized what was happening."

"That, I would have liked to see," Anna said. "Purple cows."

"The bishop was not pleased. I can tell you," Samuel said. "He had people visiting from Lancaster, and they asked him if his church allowed such nonsense as purple cows. Dat was in hot water at the next services."

"So, your twins come by it honest."

"That they do. But…" He exhaled slowly. "When Frieda was alive, the two of us used to talk out what should be done when the children needed a doctor or when they needed correcting. Usually, I wanted to talk to them, and Frieda was all for a good backside tanning. But my Dat was always light on the switching, and I never really got the hang of it. Now, with just me to make the decisions…I wonder if I'm too soft. If they get into even more mischief."

"Our Dat never spanked us. Aunt Martha spanked me once, but never Mam or Dat." Anna pulled a face. "I deserved it. Dorcas and I got into four plates of brownies that Aunt Martha had made for a quilting bee, and ate most of them."

"How old were you?"

"Nine." She wrinkled her nose. "We ate so many that they made us sick."

He chuckled. "So, what do you think? Should I spank Peter and Rudy? It almost seems like a spanking is getting off easy, considering how bad Martha felt. And her ruined boots. I gave her money for new ones, and I'll make the boys pay for it out of their own savings, but—"

"You're right, Samuel," she said softly. "It *is* getting off too light. They were disrespectful, and they need to learn a lesson. But I wouldn't spank them. All that proves is that you are bigger and stronger than they are, and that you have that right."

He put his elbows on the table and leaned toward her. "So what would you suggest?"

"Well…" She looked thoughtful. "Since it was manure that caused the trouble, it might be good to send them over to clean Aunt Martha's stable after school every day for a week. They should pay for the boots, and they should apologize to her. But hard work never hurt anybody. And spending time mucking stalls will be time they can spend thinking on how they can be better behaved children."

"Martha expected me to give them a sound thrashing. Reuben, too. They said as much when they left. 'Spare the rod and spoil the child', Reuben said. He is our preacher."

"True," Anna agreed. "He is, but *you* are their

father. It is *your* responsibility to guide your children and teach them. You have to do what you think is right."

He nodded. "Cleaning out Martha's stable, that's a good idea. And maybe her henhouse as well. Two boys, two chores."

"And a proper apology," Anna reminded him. "They have to do that. It's important a boy learns to apologize for his failings. Learning as a child makes it easier as an adult."

He sighed audibly with relief. It was a good decision. "You are wise beyond your years," he pronounced.

Anna blushed as she reached for his empty plate. "It makes me feel better, to hear what you think."

"But you knew a spanking wouldn't suit. You didn't need me to tell you that."

"I worry that my heart is too soft," he admitted. "And sometimes with boys, a man must be hard."

"But not too hard," she said with a smile.

"You see, this is why I think we should court. You and I, we make a good team. We would make a good marriage," he said, sitting up straight and looking into her eyes. "I won't change my mind."

"But I haven't said yes," she reminded him. "And I have until my birthday to come up with an answer."

"It will have to do," he answered. "And now, I

should get home. But you have helped me, eased my mind about Rudy and Peter."

She followed him to the door and stood there watching him as he walked to his buggy. Snow was falling again, and darkness was closing in on the farmyard. "The pie was good," he said.

"Danke." She smiled and waved, then closed the door.

As he drove down the Yoder lane, Samuel wondered if it had been the smartest thing for him to come by buggy. The road would be slick, and he would have to be cautious about traffic. Some of the Englishers drove like drunken chickens on ice, and not all knew how to safely share the highway with horse-drawn vehicles. He turned on his battery-powered lights and guided the gelding onto the blacktop.

Only two cars passed before Samuel drew alongside the chair shop. Near the mailbox, he caught sight of Roman clearing snow away from the driveway. Roman called out to him and waved. Samuel wanted to get home, but Roman was his friend, and he might need something.

"Some weather, eh?" Samuel said as he reined in the horse. He'd pulled into the parking area, well off the road. "Think we'll get much more tonight?"

"Ya." Roman leaned on his shovel. "Weatherman on the radio says maybe two inches."

"Not too much." He waited. Roman had something on his mind; he could tell. Roman wasn't one to keep a man from his evening chores without reason. "Something?" Samuel asked. "Is there a problem?"

"I don't know," Roman answered. "Word is, you're courting one of the Yoder girls. Noodle said—"

"Noodle Troyer talks too much."

"So you're not? Nothing to it?"

Samuel leaned forward and rested his elbow on the dashboard. "I want to court Anna, but she's not certain she'll have me."

"Anna, then, is it? Not Hannah?"

Samuel chuckled. "It was never Hannah. I think the world of Hannah, you know that. Who wouldn't? She's a good woman, but I'm set on Anna."

"It's a lot, asking a girl that young to take on a ready-made family." Roman leaned the shovel handle against the mailbox and came over to the buggy. "She's a hardworker, Anna. None better. But the age difference between you might be too much. Those twins of yours are a handful."

Samuel stroked his chin. "Not something I haven't wrestled with, Roman. It's time I took another wife, and she seems to me to be the best fit. I'd treat her right, be good to her."

Roman looked thoughtful.

"You have problems with that?" Samuel asked. "You think I'm too old for her?"

"*Ne.* It's just that…" Roman tugged at his knit hat. "Frieda was a real looker, and Anna…Anna's a special girl. I wouldn't want to see her hurt."

Samuel tensed. "No more than I would. I wouldn't ask her if I thought to make her second-best. I've prayed over it."

"Have you thought of talking it over with the bishop?"

Samuel shook his head. "I have a lot of respect for Atlee, but I didn't pick his wife for him, and I'd not think to ask him about choosing mine."

A grin split Roman's face, and he nodded. "Fair enough. It's none of my business either, I suppose, but Jonas was my friend. If he was here, he'd be askin' these questions. No offense meant."

"And none taken. But in the end, it's between Anna and me."

"You spoke to Hannah, asked her blessing?"

"I made it clear to her how I feel about Anna. They didn't want anything said, not until Anna is sure, but it sounds like the whole community is already buzzing."

Roman chuckled. "Martha and Reuben are buzzin', for sure. Reuben told Noodle he thought you'd had your eye on his Dorcas."

"Nothing wrong with Dorcas, other than her mother, but she's not right for me. Anna's the one."

"And if she turns you down?"

"She won't," Samuel said with more conviction than he felt. "And if she does, I'll just have to talk a little harder to convince her to change her mind."

Chapter Nine

Three days passed, and Anna was no closer to coming to a decision concerning her dilemma. In truth, she hadn't had much time to think, because Grossmama's arrival had thrown the entire house into a tizzy. The Yoder household had gone from four members to eight overnight, meaning more laundry, larger meals and generally more confusion as to who would tackle which tasks. Not that it was all bad. Having Rebecca and Leah home again was wonderful, and they'd sat up until nearly eleven every night talking, so late that Susanna usually fell asleep before they got her to bed. There had been little quiet time for Anna to consider whether or not to allow Samuel to court her.

"This oatmeal is lumpy. And it has too much salt," Grossmama's piercing voice cut through Anna's musing as she carried a plate of blueberry pancakes to the kitchen table. "I think your mother is trying to poison me," Grossmama fretted.

"Ne," Aunt Jezebel soothed. "Hannah wouldn't do that, Sister. She's done everything possible to make us feel at home."

"Well, I'm *not* at home," Grossmama said. "My back hurts. That bed is too hard, and there's a bathroom next to it. All night long, the water keeps running. Swish-slosh. Swish-slosh. A body can't get a wink of sleep."

Anna laid a gentle hand on her grandmother's shoulder. "I know you must miss your own house, but Mam really wants you to be happy here with us."

"I'm happy." Susanna slid her chair over close to Grossmama's. "'Member when you made me gingerbread? When I was little?"

Anna's grandmother reached for a pancake and then another. Aunt Jezebel lifted the pitcher of syrup to pour it onto the pancakes, but Grossmama snapped at her. *"Ne.* I want honey on my cakes." She looked around suspiciously. "Did Hannah make them?"

"Anna," Susanna said. "Anna did."

Grossmama was already chewing. "Dry," she muttered. "Too dry."

Leah brought the honey jar. "You'll like this," she said. "Apple blossom honey from Johanna's hives."

"Don't be so sure." Grossmama took a noisy

slurp of coffee. "Where's Hannah? She shouldn't be lazin' in bed at this hour."

"Mam's already gone," Anna said. "Remember? Mam teaches school."

"Where's my Jonas? Hannah should see he has a decent breakfast before she goes out visiting."

Leah arched an eyebrow. "Um, Dat's milking," she murmured, cutting her eyes at Anna.

"What? Speak up, girl!"

"Leah, why don't you grab some more plates? Johanna will be here soon with the children," Anna said.

"Johanna wants you to teach her how you make your rugs," Aunt Jezebel explained to her sister. "Everyone thinks you make the best rugs."

"Better than Hannah's," Grossmama said. "That one by my bed is all uneven braids and loose stitches. Hannah is a slow learner. I don't know how Jonas puts up with her."

"Mam found a length of lovely blue cotton cloth at Spence's," Anna said. "It will go perfectly with the yellow that Aunt Jezebel showed me. Johanna wants to make a rug for Baby Katie's room."

"Hmmp." Grossmama snorted. "A fine thing, when your mother can go sashshaying off wherever she pleases and leave Jonas without his breakfast." She stabbed another pancake. "I'm going home to Ohio after dinner. The weather here is too cold for my arthritis."

"It was colder at home," Aunt Jezebel reminded her.

"I don't care. I'm going as soon as Jonas hitches up my buggy."

"You haven't even had time to visit with your family, yet," Anna said. "Aunt Alma and Aunt Martha and their families would be disappointed if you went home so soon."

Grossmama belched, pushing away from the table. "Those pancakes are dry as corn husks." She looked at Anna. "Why would I want to see them? Mean-spirited girls, both of them. If Martha smiled once, her back teeth would fall out."

Leah choked back a strangled giggle.

"Come sit in the rocking chair by the window and watch for Johanna, Grossmama," Anna suggested. "You can look at all the pretty snow."

"Nothing pretty about snow," she snapped, slowing rising from the table. "Makes my hands ache."

Anna sighed. There was a lot to do today. She wanted to bake a ham for the evening meal and make cookies for Samuel's children. She hoped that things would get easier with Grossmama after she settled in. Leah and Rebecca had kept her up late last night, telling her tales of their grandmother's outrageous behavior.

Sometimes Grossmama was almost pleasant and sharp in her mind, and the next minute she lost track of reality. According to Leah, Grossmama frequently hid her change purse or her belongings and forgot where she put them. Then she would insist that Aunt Jezebel was stealing from her. And even though Dat had been gone more than two years, Grossmama believed that he was still alive. At first, the sisters had tried gently to remind her of the truth, but Hannah had suggested letting the matter go. With Grossmama's mind as it was, each time she was told her son was dead, it was if she had to relive it all over again. Sometimes an unclear mind could be a blessing, Mam told them.

It hurt Anna when Grossmama said mean things about Mam, when she was always so good to her. The two of them had always rubbed each other like a blister in new leather shoes. Grossmama hadn't wanted Dat to marry Mam because she'd been raised Mennonite.

Ruth said that she doubted anyone would have been good enough to marry Lovina's only son. And Grossmama didn't get along any better with her own daughters. She certainly didn't make her sister, Jezebel's, life easy either, but Anna knew in her heart that there was good in her grandmother. Lovina had a lifetime of wisdom and experience to share, and no one made a finer braided rug.

Anna rested her hand on the back of the rocker as Grossmama sat down, and she handed her a shawl. It was warm in the kitchen, but the shawl seemed to make Lovina feel safe, so Anna always kept it nearby.

Respect and caring for older people had been ingrained in Anna since she was a small child. She felt deeply that providing food and shelter and medical care wasn't enough. It was important to make Grossmama a part of the household, to show her that she was loved and wanted. The question was—how?

Church was held every other Sunday. This week, Sunday was a day of rest, a day for visiting with friends and family, for reading the Bible and for remembering the blessings that the Lord provided. Leah, Rebecca and Susanna were just clearing away the dishes from the noon meal when Samuel arrived at the kitchen door with his three girls.

"Come in," Mam said. "Anna, look who's here."

Anna offered Samuel a nervous smile. She could feel her face growing hot as Leah gave her a knowing look and Rebecca kicked her ankle under the table. Grossmama and Aunt Jezebel, still seated at the table, stared. Irwin scooped up Jeremiah and fled the kitchen for the back of the house.

"You've come to see Hannah?" Grossmama asked. "Not wise. She's not a good cook."

"Sister," Aunt Jezebel chided. "Hannah is a fine cook."

Lori Ann giggled and Mae pulled off a wet mitten and stuck her thumb in her mouth. Samuel took a deep breath, and his handsome face grew ruddy. "*Ne,* Lovina. I've come to see Anna."

"Anna? Why?" Grossmama asked.

Susanna piped up. "Samuel's courting Anna."

Anna rushed to take the little girls' coats. Samuel hung his on the hook on the back of the kitchen door. "Susanna," Anna said. "There's a new copy of *Family Life* that Naomi might like to read, and maybe you could take Lori Ann and Mae up to the attic and let them play with the Noah's Ark." She looked at Samuel, nervous, but a little excited, too. He'd come to see her, just her. This was one of the ways couples got to know each other when they were courting. And even though she and Samuel weren't courting, the idea caused a flutter in her stomach. "Would you like to sit in the parlor? Irwin made a fire in the stove this morning."

Samuel nodded, and Anna led the way to a small room that was only used when special guests came to call. A high-backed oak bench that had been made in Lancaster more than a hundred years ago, three cane-seat chairs and a larger mahogany

Windsor chair were arranged around the cast-iron stove. The walls were a soft cream and the wide chair rail and molding were dove-white. More straight-back chairs lined the wall and the worn plank floor was clean enough to eat off.

On the dark oak table lay Dat's Old German Bible and a newer one belonging to her mother. Other hymnals, Bibles and histories of the Amish martyrs lined the shelves of a simple oak bookcase that Eli had built. Anna opened the interior shutters, so that light poured through the tall windows from Mam's flower garden and motioned Samuel to take the single armchair.

Instead, he pushed the heavy pocket door nearly closed, leaving only a few inches open, for propriety's sake, settled onto the bench and patted the seat beside him. "I think that you could sit beside me, Anna. Your mother, Grossmama and sisters are in the next room."

Hesitantly, she sat where he asked. "We're not doing a very good job of keeping this a secret," she said. Her voice came out so soft that it was a wonder Samuel heard her. Still, it wasn't unpleasant sitting so close to him.

"You don't have to be afraid of me."

"I'm not afraid." That wasn't exactly true. She was afraid, afraid that this would all come to nothing, that her deepest wish might be nothing more than a girl's silly daydreaming. Shivers ran under her skin and her heart raced and skipped.

"I know you asked for more time," Samuel said, "but—"

"Dat! Mae—Mae—Mae wet her pants." Lori Ann squeezed through the opening in the doorway. "She made a—a—a puddle on the floor. Sh-sh-she did."

Samuel started to rise, but Anna halted him with a hand on his arm. "It's nothing, Samuel. You don't have to worry yourself over a child's accident."

He relaxed, giving a hesitant smile. "Usually I do."

"Not here. We're used to such things." She waved to Lori Ann. "Ask Mam to come if Susanna can't find dry clothes for her." The little girl nodded and dashed off. Anna looked back into Samuel's face, thinking again how big he was, how handsome. "This is your day of rest, too. You should make the best of it."

He smiled and nodded. "Being with you is restful, Anna." He hesitated. "I…I told Roman," he admitted.

"Oh." She exhaled slowly.

"He's my friend. I wanted him to know that we were thinking of…" He reached for her hand and cradled it in his broad one. "I wanted him to know that I'd asked to court you—that I want you to be my wife."

Anna closed her eyes, savoring the warmth of his touch. She hoped that Samuel wouldn't think she was fast. Handholding was allowed between couples that were walking out together, which they weren't, but Samuel seemed so sure. And, as he had said, her mother was nearby. Her throat constricted. She wanted to ask what Roman had thought, but the words wouldn't come. Instead, she breathed in the clean male scent of Samuel, picturing in her mind him forking hay and hitching up the horse. All her life, she'd felt too big. Next to Samuel, she didn't seem nearly as tall or broad.

"Anna, I think maybe we—"

The door scraped against the floor. There was the tap-tap of Grossmama's cane, and the old woman shuffled into the room, followed by Aunt Jezebel. Grossmama stared at them for a long minute, then took a chair near the stove, directly across from Samuel and Anna, and blew her nose loudly on a big handkerchief.

"Sister wanted to join you," Aunt Jezebel said apologetically, as she took a seat in one of the cane chairs. "She insisted."

"You courting my Anna?" Grossmama demanded.

"Ya," Samuel answered. He released Anna's hand and she tucked it safely under her apron. She saw by Aunt Jezebel's expression that she'd noticed, but Anna wasn't certain that Grossmama had seen them holding hands.

"Ne," Anna said. "Maybe. We're not sure."

Her grandmother ignored her and looked hard at Samuel. "Good. She's a good girl. Make you a good wife." She frowned and blew her nose again. "But first you ask my Jonas for permission. Ask her father. My son."

A furrow appeared between Samuel's brows, and he glanced at Anna in confusion. Anna's eyes widened and she nodded.

"I will," he said.

"Is right. Proper," Grossmama said. "My Jonas is a bishop. He has a good farm. *Ya?"*

Samuel nodded. "A very good farm."

"Do you have a job?" Grossmama asked. "Do you work hard? Let me see your hands."

Dutifully, Samuel got up, walked over to her and held out his hands. Grossmama stared.

"Turn them over." When he did as he was told, the old woman nodded. "Strong hands. Not lazy hands. Is a good man, Anna. You take him." Grossmama twisted to look at Aunt Jezebel. "Well, are you going to read to me or not? I can't find my glasses. I think Hannah took them."

"I don't believe Mam took your glasses," Anna said, rising to her feet. She walked to Samuel and whispered. "This isn't going to work. Let's go back in the kitchen."

"What?" Grossmama demanded. She peered at

Samuel. "He doesn't work? No good. How will he feed your babies?"

Anna felt a flush start at her chest and flash over her neck and face. Her cheeks were burning as she motioned toward the door. "Kitchen," she begged Samuel. And then to Grossmama she said, "Samuel has the farm behind ours. Where the school is. Fine fields and a big herd of milk cows. He can provide for a family."

"My Jonas is milking the cows," she replied. "Go ask him now, young man. It's only right."

Anna fled the room with Samuel on her heels. "Grossmama thinks—" she began when they were safely in the next room with the sliding pocket door closed behind them.

"Is all right. I have a great uncle who thinks he is married to two women." Samuel chuckled. "He's a hundred and two."

"Is he?" Anna asked. "Married to two women?"

"Uncle Jay? He was married four times, but all of them have passed on." His grin grew wider. "He insists he's married to his preacher's wife and an English woman who keeps the corner store."

"She doesn't mean harm," Anna explained, standing in the hall beside him. "Dat was her only son. I think it's easier for her to let her go on thinking he's still alive."

"Your grossmama doesn't frighten me," he said.

"I like her. And she's a smart woman. She said I would be a good husband for you."

"I have not said yes, Samuel."

"But you will." He reached for her hand and she put it behind her. "It's just a matter of time. We will stand before the church together, Anna."

"We'll see about that." Her stomach felt as though she'd eaten an entire shoo-fly pie and then rolled down Charley's father's steep hill. Breathless, she led the way into the kitchen where Mam, Rebecca, Leah and Samuel's three girls were baking cookies. Irwin sat on the floor near the stove, pulling an empty spool on a string of yarn for Jeremiah to chase. Irwin had used a pen to make eyes on the spool, hoping the little terrier would take the toy for a mouse.

"Not much chance to talk alone with her, is there?" Mam asked with a chuckle. Samuel shook his head. "Maybe the two of you should walk across the field to Ruth and Eli's. Visit with them. I'm sure Ruth has the coffeepot on and they'd appreciate the company."

"It would be nice to visit with Ruth and Eli and Miriam and Charley," Samuel agreed. "But I'm not sure I should drop in with all my girls."

Naomi laid the cookbook on the table and glanced back at her father. Her glasses were smudged with flour, but she was smiling. "We're making sugar cookies, Dat. They aren't ready yet, but Hannah said we could take them home."

"Why don't you go on?" Leah said. "We'll watch them. It will give the two of you a chance to talk."

"Alone." Rebecca giggled. "Since you're courting."

"We *aren't* courting," Anna corrected.

Samuel shrugged. "I'm courting her. We're just waiting to see if she—"

"You should take her to the taffy pulling at Johanna's Wednesday night," Leah suggested excitedly. "Anna's never had a fellow take her to a young people's get-together."

"Taffy pulling?" Samuel looked unconvinced. "Will it be all the younger folk?"

"Oh, Samuel, I meant to ask," Anna said, all in a rush. Suddenly she wanted to go to the frolic, and she wanted to go with him. "I would like that."

"Then it's settled," Leah said, clapping her hands together. "Anna should have fun, and you can always just watch, Samuel, if you don't want to pull taffy."

Mam was handing Samuel his coat. "Now you two go on. It's broad daylight. You can certainly walk to Anna's sister's house without causing talk in the neighborhood."

Samuel nodded. "If you're sure the girls won't be a trouble."

"The girls will be fine. I'm sure Charley will

want to show off those new animals he bought at the auction. And you and Eli always get on well together."

"Anna?" Samuel looked at her, accepting his coat. "Do you want to walk to your sister's? It's cold out, and your feet—"

"I would like that, Samuel," Anna interrupted happily. "And I have new boots. I'm not afraid of a little snow."

Soon, the two of them were crossing the farmyard. Samuel's horse looked up from the shelter of the shed and whinnied. "I'll be back for you," he promised the animal.

"See you in an hour or so," Mam called from the porch.

Samuel waved and then he slowed his steps so that Anna could keep up. "I never thought this courting stuff would be so hard," he confided to her.

"Because you are older than me?" she asked.

He shook his head, stuffing his hands into the pockets of his sturdy denim coat. "Because I've never done it before. My mother and father and Frieda's parents arranged my marriage. We didn't have to sit in the parlor across from old grandmothers or go to taffy pulls."

She felt a stab of disappointment. "You don't want to go. It's all right. We don't have to—"

"Ne." He stopped and faced her. "We will go.

You deserve to do these things, Anna. If this is going to work, we'll both have to make compromises. If you can, I can."

"Compromises." She sighed. "We need to make compromises."

"And I will keep praying. As I told Roman, if God wants this match, nothing can keep us apart."

Nothing but me, Anna thought, as all her old fears and feelings of inadequacy bubbled up inside her.

He looped her arm through his and they began to walk side-by-side down the lane. "You're the woman for me, Anna Yoder," he continued. "And I'll do whatever I have to, so that you will see the right of it."

Chapter Ten

Wednesday night's taffy pulling at Johanna's was every bit as uncomfortable for Samuel as he thought it would be. Giggling teenage girls and immature boys, like Elmer Beachy and Harvey Bontrager, did their best to attract attention with silly pranks and jokes. Donald Zook shook a bottle of soda pop and sprayed two of the girls, causing shrieks, and dashed around the kitchen, making Johanna threaten him with expulsion from the frolic if he didn't behave.

There were only a few young women of Anna's age. Leah, Rebecca, Miriam, Ruth and Susanna were present, but Ruth and Miriam were both married. Anna's cousin Dorcas was older than Anna, but she seemed no more an adult than the sixteen-year-olds. Although Samuel enjoyed every bite of the homemade donuts Anna brought, the entire candy-making evening seemed more suited to fun for his children than for teenagers.

It was little wonder that Samuel felt out of place. After all, he was a deacon of the church and an authority figure. It was obvious that the young people didn't want him here anymore than he wanted to be here. But Anna didn't seem to notice that the kids were obviously subdued by his presence. She appeared to be having a good time, and that was why he had come. Why she'd wanted to be here, he didn't know. She seemed a woman grown next to these kids.

According to custom, Samuel hadn't brought her to the taffy pull, she'd come with her sisters. Usually, girls traveled to singings and frolics with their family members or friends. And if a boy asked a girl and she liked him, the two would quietly slip out of the house and ride home together.

Some Amish parents were liberal. Once they reached the girl's house, the pair might be allowed to sit up late in the parlor, talking or playing Dutch Blitz or other approved games. These dates were much less serious than courting, and were considered an accepted part of social life for those in their late teens.

Samuel was glad that he'd have a few more years with his own children before they entered their *running around* period. Other, more liberal churches allowed their young people a time of *Rumspringa,* when they were expected to experience some of the loose behavior of the English world. That was not the case here in Kent County. Thankfully, the bishops, preachers and congregation agreed that such freedom opened their children to too many dangers.

But as for himself, he was thirty-seven, a mature man with a family and responsibilities. And sitting at Johanna's table with buttered hands pulling taffy with Anna was a far distance from where he wanted to be. He'd long outgrown the taste for moon pies and popcorn balls, let alone the sweet bottled grape soda the kids seemed to favor.

Samuel wondered if he'd have been wiser to have simply refused to come. And for the first time, a small doubt crept into his mind. Maybe courting a younger woman would be more of a task than he'd thought. Would Anna expect him to keep her company at the young people's singings and game nights?

He wondered if Hannah would allow him to come in and spend time alone with Anna tonight—provided there was any privacy in the Yoder household. He wanted to relax, to talk over his day with Anna, to just sit and look at her without being watched and judged by her family. He had liked the feel of her smaller, warm hand in his, and he longed to put his arm around her and sit beside her with her head on his shoulder. He wanted to inhale the scent of her hair and stare into her beautiful cinnamon-colored eyes. Oh, he was smitten, no doubt about it. He wanted to take Anna as his wife. But so far she'd kept him hanging, and the longer she hesitated to give him an answer, the greater his feelings for her grew.

As soon as Anna's pieces of taffy were stretched thin enough to suit her and were ready for cutting, Samuel excused himself and went out to the barn. Johanna's husband was there in his workshop, and Samuel thought that he could better spend his time having a long-needed discussion with Wilmer. Wilmer worked long hours on his construction job and often was away for days at a time. Although working close to home was best, Samuel couldn't fault the man for providing for Johanna and their two small children.

As he approached the workshop, Samuel caught the smell of tobacco. Wilmer had originally come from Kentucky, where some of the Amish still grew tobacco as a cash crop. Again, Samuel didn't want to judge. He'd experimented with smoking a pipe as a young man before he joined the church, but the practice was generally frowned upon. His role in the community as a deacon was as advisor and counselor, but he couldn't insist that Wilmer give up his cigars. That was between Wilmer and his conscience.

"Run you out, did they?" Wilmer looked up from the chain saw he'd been oiling. "Never expected you to last this long with those crazy kids."

"I feel a lot more at ease here in the barn," Samuel agreed.

"Bunch of nonsense, I say, but Johanna would have it."

"You know how young folks are. They need a little clean fun now and then. And Johanna and her sisters are a good example for the girls."

Wilmer grunted and reached for his half-smoked cigar. He took a long puff and blew smoke through his nose. "I'd offer you a stogie, but I don't suppose you use tobacco."

"I gave it up a long time ago," Samuel answered. "Never missed it, either."

"Well, to each his own, I suppose." Wilmer waved toward an overturned peach basket and Samuel sat down on it. "'Spose you're courting one of those Yoder girls. Can't figure any other reason you'd be out on such a cold night."

"I've a mind to have Anna."

"Anna?"

"*Ya,* Anna. We suit each other."

Wilmer made a sound of disapproval. "You'd do well to stay away from any of them, if you ask me. Hannah's too liberal. She spoiled the lot of them, and Jonas—when he was alive—wasn't much better. They don't know their proper place. Too mouthy for womenfolk."

"Not that I've seen. Hannah's always seemed

sensible to me. She does a good job with her farm, and the school's never had a better teacher."

"That's what I'm talkin' about. The bishop shouldn't allow it. A widow's got no business workin' outside the house. She ought to have enough to do at home."

"She needs the salary from teaching to help support her family," Samuel defended.

Wilmer snorted. "Should have remarried…long ago. The Bible says that a man is the head of the house. You know what I think? I think Hannah Yoder likes fillin' a man's shoes. She wasn't born Old Order, you know. Raised Mennonite. She's not Plain, and never will be as far as I can see."

Samuel shifted on his basket. Talking about Hannah like this wasn't right, but Wilmer was family and he wasn't. Not yet, at least. Still, he didn't like what Wilmer had to say. He was beginning to think he was more uncomfortable in the barn than in the kitchen. He needed to turn the conversation to Wilmer, and he needed to do it without offending him. "Hannah is outspoken, that's true," he admitted, "but we've never had a cross word, and she's been good to my kids."

"You're not careful, she'll let them run as wild as she does Jonah when he's at her place. My girl, now, Katy, she's a sweet baby, but Johanna and her mother will ruin Jonah, given half a chance."

Samuel knew Wilmer and Johanna's boy, a

sturdy, ginger-haired lad, somewhere between the age of his own Mae and Lori Ann. The child had always been well behaved at church services, which was more than he could say for his own kids. Maybe if Wilmer had to father Rudy and Peter for a few weeks, he wouldn't be so quick to fault little Jonah. But Jonah was Wilmer's boy, and telling a man he was too hard on his own child wouldn't make Wilmer any more likely to hear what else he had to say.

A single kerosene lantern gave off a yellow, wavering circle of light. Samuel noted that the bench was littered with tools and wire and bits of this and that. He hadn't been in Wilmer's shop in two years, but it had been a lot neater then. Wilmer had a lot of expensive saws and woodworking equipment, but careless treatment had left many rusting and gathering dust.

"We missed you at services the last two church Sundays," Samuel said.

Wilmer concentrated on wiping the grease off his chain saw with a dirty rag. "Had something more important to do."

"Nothing is more important than worship, Wilmer. If your spirit's heavy, it's best to go and talk to someone."

"You?"

"Me. One of the elders, or maybe our bishop. Atlee's a sensible man with the gift of sharing the

Holy Word. There's nothing you carry in your heart that can't be eased by the Lord."

Noodle Troyer had told Samuel that he'd seen Wilmer coming out of a package store last Sunday with a bottle of what could only be spirits. And word was that some had seen Wilmer driving his horse and buggy home from Dover after dark on a work night in less than a sober state. Samuel didn't want to mention the alcohol. If Wilmer had a drinking problem, it was more than a deacon could handle. It would take the preachers, Bishop Atlee and the elders to help him. But the matter of Wilmer not attending church services, that was Samuel's responsibility.

Wilmer turned to give him a long stare. "Sometimes a man has worries that plague him like mange on a dog. No matter how hard you try to ease it, the itch is still there."

"All the more reason to take it to the Lord in prayer," Samuel said. "And to reach out to the church elders for help. None of us can make it through the trials of this world alone."

"Easy for you to say, Samuel. Farm the size of yours, big herd of milk cows. You've always been a lucky man. Not me. I work hard, but everything I touch turns to empty husks."

"How can you say that? You've got a good wife, two healthy children, steady work and a community that cares about you."

Wilmer's eyes narrowed. "You notice the color of my baby girl's hair?"

"Brown?" Samuel didn't know what Wilmer was getting at.

"Real dark, dark like mine. And the boy's hair is red."

"Like Johanna's. All the Yoder girls are gingers like their father."

"Umm." Wilmer grunted again and turned back to his chain saw. There was silence for a few minutes until he glanced back. "She had to have one of those C-sections when Jonah was born. Where they cut the woman open to get the baby out. I expect I'll be paying off that bill until he's old enough to start school."

Samuel remembered Johanna's emergency delivery. Since their people carried no insurance, like the English did, the church had rallied to help the young family with the expense of Jonah's medical bills. They'd held breakfasts and suppers and even a benefit auction. At the time, Samuel thought that the majority of the bill had been paid.

Maybe he was wrong. If it was money trouble that was worrying Wilmer, that was something that the community could do something about. Samuel would take it up with the bishop when next he saw him. Whether it was help for a barn raising or illness, the members of the church joined hands to assist their own.

"I'm sorry to hear that you're having a hard time," Samuel said. "You should have spoke up sooner." He stood up. The frolic would be winding down, and he wanted to get back in to Anna. "The church is here for you. I'm here for you."

"Are you?" Wilmer's tone was flat. "Heard you're killing hogs next week. If you want to help, send over one. My smokehouse is as empty as last summer's jelly jars."

"A pig?" Samuel nodded. "I'll be glad to let you have one. I'll send the boys over with the meat right after butchering."

"Obliged."

As Samuel walked away, he wondered why Wilmer's request made him uneasy. The gift of a hog to a neighbor in need was something that he'd done before without a moment's hesitation. Was it that he'd never particularly taken to Johanna's husband? The Bible said to love thy neighbor, but even a devout man couldn't be expected to like everyone. And he certainly didn't begrudge Johanna and the children a stock of winter's meat. He'd donate the pig and a front quarter of beef to the family, and he'd pray for Wilmer as well.

"He don't look nothin' like my girl," Wilmer called after him. "The boy. Jonah. Not like any of my kin."

Samuel shook his head and walked on. It wouldn't

hurt to ask the Lord for a change in his own attitude. He needed patience and he needed to be more charitable.

Inside Johanna's house, Dorcas followed Anna into the bathroom and closed the door. The two washed the sticky candy off their hands, reached for the towel at the same time and laughed. "Share and share alike," Anna said.

"Are you riding home with him?" Dorcas asked in a low voice. On the far side of the door they heard one of the Beachy girls teasing Harvey and giggling.

"With who?"

"Who do you think? Samuel. That big barn of a man you had pulling taffy with you."

"Ya," Anna admitted. "I like him, Dorcas. I like him a lot."

"I know you do," Dorcas whispered. "But it still worries me. I'm sorry that Mam did what she did, going to his house. She deserved what the twins did to her. Sometimes I'd like to do worse."

Anna had to work hard not to smile. "I think she means well."

"Maybe, but it doesn't seem like it to me." Dorcas hung up the towel. "She told Samuel that I'd be a better match for him—right in front of me. I could have sunk through your mother's kitchen floor."

Anna put her arm around Dorcas and hugged her. "Samuel would know it didn't come from you."

"I wouldn't want this to come between us, Anna. Even if you do marry him."

"It won't. You're my best friend and you always will be."

Dorcas nodded. "I still think this is a bad idea."

Anna swallowed, trying to dissolve the lump in her throat. "But you said...you said you'd jump at the chance to have someone like Samuel. Why shouldn't I let him court me if he really wants to? It would be wonderful, living close to Mam and my sisters, having my own home...taking care of Samuel and his family."

Someone banged on the bathroom door. "Just a minute," Dorcas said. She grabbed Anna's hand and squeezed it. "Do you think Samuel fit in here tonight?"

Anna's shook her head. "Not really. It was easy to see that he wanted to get away. Most everyone here is too young for him."

"Exactly. So why would he pick you? Have you thought that maybe he's still in love with his wife, that he's only asked you so he'll have someone to take her place, someone who's willing to work hard...and..."

"And what?" Anna asked. She'd been having such a good time tonight. She knew that Samuel had only come to please her. She was looking forward to having him drive her home in his buggy, maybe asking him in for coffee and a slice of her chocolate pie. But Dorcas's doubts brought her own back. Maybe her cousin was right. "You may as well say it all."

Dorcas took a deep breath. "What if he's marrying you because he knows he could never really love you? If he wants a companion, but not a wife in that way? If he thinks of you as…well, a sister?"

"A sister?" Anna bit her bottom lip. "You think Samuel thinks of me as a sister?" Suddenly a black hole seemed to open below her feet. "I…didn't think that a man like Samuel would ever want me," she murmured. "But he wouldn't take no for an answer. I prayed over it, and it seemed to me that it was the right thing to consider his offer."

"So you don't care *why* he wants to marry you?"

"Hurry up in there," came a boy's voice. "I drank three sodas."

"You hush that talk," Dorcas hollered. "We'll be done when we're done."

"Of course I care," Anna whispered. "I don't think of him as a brother." Had she been fooling herself? Anna turned back and looked into the small mirror, and the same, round pudding face stared back. *Why would he want a fat girl?* How did she know if this was the way it was done…how Samuel would act if he really cared for her? She'd never been courted before. "He tried to hold my hand on Sunday."

"Doesn't mean anything. Friends hold hands."

"Not men and women friends."

"Did you let him?"

"Ne." Anna choked on the lie. *"Ya,* but just for a minute."

"Hmm." Dorcas folded her arms over her chest. "I don't know what that means. Maybe he does like you." But Anna didn't think Dorcas sounded convinced. "Is he driving you home?"

"I think so. He hasn't asked me yet."

"Dorcas!"

"We'd better go," Anna said.

"Tell me everything tomorrow. Then we can decide what to do." Dorcas opened the door and Elmer Beachy rushed past them into the bathroom.

What do you mean "we"? Anna thought as they rejoined the others in the kitchen. She valued her cousin's advice, but Dorcas had never been courted either. This was all too confusing. If Johanna didn't have a houseful, she might have asked for her guidance. Ruth and Miriam had both recently courted and married, but they hadn't married older men, as Johanna had. Actually, the difference between Johanna and Wilmer wasn't as great as that between her and Samuel, but Johanna might have some good ideas. She would listen to everything Anna had to say and give her opinion. And she didn't care if it was what you wanted to hear or not. Next to Mam, Johanna gave the best advice. And Anna really needed some. She'd been about to tell Samuel he could court her, and now she was more in a quandary than ever.

Chapter Eleven

A half hour later, Anna found herself bundled into Samuel's buggy with a sheepskin robe over her lap, riding down Johanna's driveway. Her sisters, just ahead of them, turned left toward home. Samuel guided the horse right.

"Where are you going?" Anna asked him. "Home is that way."

Samuel chuckled. "I think I know where you live." He grinned boyishly at her in the light of the carriage lamps. "The rules say that I'm supposed to drive my girl home. They don't say what route I have to take to get there."

"Mam won't be pleased," Anna ventured. Sitting beside him was wonderful, but the doubts and fears that Dorcas had raised made her apprehensive. She wanted to come right out and ask Samuel if this was a courting of convenience, or something more...but she couldn't be that bold. And if he said that he thought of her as a good companion and nothing more, she couldn't stand it.

Anna's stomach churned. She shouldn't have eaten that second popcorn ball or the whoopie pie. She should have stuck to the apple and celery slices that everyone was dipping in peanut butter. No wonder she was so fat and ugly. She always had a good appetite. And what man wanted a wife who could lift a hundred-pound bag of calf feed? She sank back on the seat and clutched the bag of taffy she was saving for Samuel's children.

"Are you going to invite me in when we get to your house?" he asked.

She didn't know. She hadn't decided yet. Instead of answering his question, she thrust the bag of candy toward him. "For your kids," she said.

"Danke." He took the taffy and thrust it into a compartment under the seat. "It's thoughtful of you. They love sweets. Homemade are best. They always beg for candies at Byler's store, but I don't buy much. I don't want them to have bad teeth."

Anna nodded. This was a much safer subject. *"Ya.* You are a wise father. You should see what some of the children bring to school in their lunch pails. Mam can't believe it. Cans of soda pop. Candy bars and potato chips. Not what she packed for us when we went there."

"Sandwiches and apples?"

"Sometimes. Usually cheese or meat, whatever

she had on hand. Always fruit. And in the winter we had thermoses of hot soup. Mam was big on soup and raw vegetables. I ate so many carrots when I was little that it's a wonder my ears didn't grow like a rabbit's."

"But you have nice teeth. White. Even. I always liked your teeth."

In spite of herself, Anna felt a little shiver of excitement run through her. *He liked her teeth.* She'd always brushed after the noon meal, as well as night and morning. Mam was in her forties, but she still had all of her own teeth and not a single filling. Anna wanted to be like her when she was old, and she hoped it wasn't *Hockmut* to be proud of her smile. "Mam always took us to the dentist to have our teeth cleaned."

"That's important." He shook the lines over the horse's back and the stocky Morgan turned off the blacktop road onto a dirt lane that ran through Stutzman's woods.

"Oh." Anna swallowed. Trees closed over their heads, shutting out the pale winter sky. Some of the trees were pine, others hardwood. The oak and maple leaves had fallen, and the bare branches looked like ghostly fingers. "I don't like driving this way at night."

"You'll be fine. I'd never let anything or anyone harm you, Anna. Smoky's a good horse. He may not be as fancy-stepping as some of those thor-oughbred pacers, but he knows his business."

Anna glanced from the scary trees to the Morgan, noting that Samuel had covered the horse's back with a warm, quilted blanket. Not everyone thought of their animals on such a cold winter night, and it pleased her that Samuel cared about Smoky's comfort as well as hers. He was a kindhearted man…a good man. But could they be happy together?

Even in the shadowy darkness, she could see how handsome Samuel was. Among the Plain People, looks weren't supposed to matter, but you rarely saw a good-looking man with a wife who had a face like hers. "Like to like," as Aunt Martha was fond of saying. "The Lord didn't mean for an apple tree and a paw-paw to make fruit."

Anna sighed. If Samuel was an apple tree, he'd be a Jonathan or a Yellow Delicious, and she was certainly a paw-paw—big and shapeless, with-out much taste. But still, a paw-paw could enjoy the sunshine and the rain, too, couldn't it? Why couldn't she savor every moment of this night? What would it hurt to pretend that Samuel was her beau? That he *did* love her, and that he had chosen her above any other girl in the county because he wanted her to be his wife in every way the Lord intended?

The buggy wheels squeaked and squished in the

snow. The harness creaked and Smoky huffed and puffed, sending plumes of white into the air in front of his head. The woods smelled wonderful: all evergreen, fresh and wintery. In some ways, the dark lane was scary, but in others it was wonderful. With Samuel beside her so tall and strong, what could hurt her? In spite of what she'd said to Samuel earlier, she was now glad he had taken the buggy this way. No matter what happened, she would have this night to remember…the night when, for a little while, she belonged to Samuel and he belonged to her.

"I wanted to ask you," he said in his quiet way, "to do me a favor."

"Anything."

"I have to go away on Friday. There's a farm auction over to Sudlersville. I thought to take the boys, but after what they did to your Aunt Martha, they don't deserve a day off from school. Me and another fellow, we have a ride in a van, but now I need someone to watch the kids. Naomi and the twins will be in school, but I was wondering if you would mind coming to the house and staying with the little ones?"

Something rustled in the bushes. Unconsciously, Anna slid closer to Samuel. "Of course I will," she said. "I'll be glad to. I promised Grossmama to take her to Byler's in the afternoon, but if it's all right with you, I can take the two girls along."

It was easier for her when they talked about homey things like the children. She could almost shut out the feeling that the space between them was charged in the same way the air felt before a lightning strike.

"To Byler's." He snorted. "Those two could have the walls down around you, if they take a mind to."

"They will not," she said firmly, aghast at the very idea. "My sisters are going, and Leah can be quite firm. I think she learned it taking care of Grossmama."

"Fine by me if they go, if you think you can handle them. It will take a load off my mind having you keep them for the day. I hear there's a small horse-drawn cultivator for sale, and it will be just the right size for Rudy and Peter."

There was a comfortable silence between them for perhaps five minutes. That was a nice thing about Samuel, Anna thought. They could ride along without talking and feel at ease. He wasn't like Charley, who always had to be explaining something or asking questions or telling jokes, and he certainly wasn't like any of the silly boys who'd been at Johanna's tonight. Dorcas had called him a big barn of a man, and it fit. He was solid and dependable, not exciting, but real. She liked him, a lot, but she didn't know if that was love she was feeling. She wanted the joy that she saw in Miriam's eyes every time she looked at her new husband, Charley.

Something about what Samuel had said about the boys not deserving to have a day off and go to the auction tugged at her thoughts. "What about Naomi?" she said, almost without realizing she'd said it out loud.

"Naomi? What about her?" Samuel sounded surprised.

"Maybe she'd like to go with you. To the auction."

"A girl? What would Naomi do at an auction?"

"Follow you around. Have you buy her lunch. Spend special time with her father. Naomi works hard. She takes care of her little sisters. She tries to keep the house clean."

"Keep her out of school?"

"You were going to take the twins out for the day, and Naomi gets all A's on her report card. She's at the top of her class. She deserves a reward."

"I doubt there'll be any other girls her age there."

"But *you'll* be there. You don't love her any less than Peter and Rudy, do you?"

"Ne." Samuel raised his voice. "Of course, not. Why would you say such a thing?"

Anna lowered her head so that he couldn't see her smile. "I know that you love all of your children equally, but it's important that *they* know it—

especially your daughters. And giving Naomi a special outing would make her happy."

"You don't approve of the way I raise my children?"

"*Ya,* Samuel, I do. I don't know of a better father." *Other than my own,* she thought, but didn't say. "You must do what you think right. It's only that…"

"Only what?"

She made her own voice soft and coaxing. "That a man has so many things on his mind, he may not remember what pleases a girlchild." Her father had always taken one of his daughters with him whenever he went somewhere, even if it was a trip to the dentist. And in a household of seven children, those special times with him stayed in her mind like treasures. "You know your Naomi best, Samuel, but I think she would like it."

"And other men? What would they think if I drag a girl along?"

Anna chuckled. "I think they will shake their heads and smile and hold their opinions, because I doubt few men would care to remark on what you do with your own children."

"Few men. But you would."

"I'm only a woman. My mind is on house and children. And I know that if you want to court me, you would have a woman who will speak her mind to you, not one who will bob her head like a nanny goat and say '*Ya*, Samuel, *ya*. Whatever you say.'"

He laughed. "I think there is more to you than I expected, Anna Yoder."

"More bad or more good?" she dared.

"That," he smiled, "I'm sure, I'll find out."

As Samuel drove the horse and buggy into the yard, he saw that the only lights visible were those in the kitchen and a single kerosene lamp in an upstairs window. "Someone's up late," he said, pointing to the second floor.

"Ne," Anna replied. "That's for me. Whenever one of us is away, we keep a lamp burning to welcome them home."

"Your sisters were in Ohio for most of a year. Did you leave a light in the window every night for them?"

Anna smiled in the darkness. "A Christmas candle that ran on batteries. Plastic. Susanna was in charge of replacing the batteries when they started to lose their power. She did a good job."

"I like that. It must make you feel good inside that someone would do such a thing." He climbed down and helped her out. The ride home hadn't gone as he'd expected. He'd enjoyed being alone with Anna, but she hadn't let him hold her hand. He'd been hoping for a kiss, but that wasn't going to happen either, so long as she hadn't agreed to seriously consider his proposal. "Are you going to ask me in?"

"*Ya*. I am. It's cold out here, and you need a cup of hot coffee before you start home. But we can only visit a little while. You have to be up early, and it's too nasty a night to keep Smoky standing out here."

"I thought I'd put him in the barn, out of the wind. I've a feed bag in the back. He can have some oats, although I'm sure he'd drink coffee if I offered it to him."

Samuel waited until Anna was safely on the porch before tending to Smoky. When he stomped his snowy boots off on the mat, shrugged off his coat and came into the warm kitchen a few moments later, he was enveloped by the odor of fresh coffee. Three mugs and a generous slice of pie waited on the table. Inwardly, he groaned. Seated at the end of the table was Anna's great aunt, Jezebel. Obviously, he and Anna would not be allowed to enjoy each other's company in private.

"Did you two enjoy your taffy pull?" Jezebel waved Samuel to the high-backed seat at the head of the table.

Samuel nodded and sat down.

"It was fun," Anna agreed. "Did the girls get home safe?"

"Your sisters? *Ya*. They went up to bed, seeing as how late it is." She pushed her glasses up off her nose and peered at Anna with a glint in her eyes. "Samuel's horse must be lame. It took the two of you a lot longer to come from Johanna's than it took your sisters."

"Oh, we came a different way," Anna said. "By the dirt lane." She glanced at Samuel. He was staring into his coffee cup and stirring hard with his spoon.

Her aunt nodded. "That explains it then. I took a long buggy ride or two in my day." She smiled and Anna smiled back, a little relieved Aunt Jezzy wasn't upset with her for dawdling with Samuel.

"Hannah, is she asleep?" Samuel took another forkful of the pie.

"Sound asleep," Aunt Jezebel said. "I'm the only night owl, beside you two youngsters. Thought I'd sit up and see how your evening was."

"I liked the candy making." Anna sat down at the table. "But some of the kids were silly, spraying soda pop and playing catch with popcorn balls. Johanna had to threaten to send some of the boys home early to get them to behave."

"And how did you put up with all that nonsense?" Aunt Jezebel looked pointedly at Samuel. He was scraping the last crumbs off the plate and washing them down with coffee.

"Anna wanted to go, so we went," he mumbled through a mouthful of pie. "It wasn't bad."

"I know just what you're thinking." The little

woman peered at him through her glasses. "You're wondering why I'm still up and keeping you from visiting with Anna."

Anna was afraid of what to think her great aunt might say next.

Samuel started to protest, but Aunt Jezebel silenced him by simply raising a tiny hand. "You're thinking it's not fair," she said, "that most of those boys got to drive a girl home and sit with her in her house in privacy. I have to say what I have to say about the two of you courting and then you won't hear any more from me on the matter, either of you."

"We're not courting," Anna protested. "At least, not yet."

"I'm courting," Samuel said. "She's the one who's undecided."

"Then it's good I say this now." Aunt Jezebel toyed with her own cup, turning it around and around. Anna knew her aunt was fond of spinning things; she usually made three circles before she was satisfied. "I know you might think we're being overprotective of Anna. Maybe watching over her closer than her sisters might have been watched." She tapped a finger on the table. Three times. "I don't want you to take it personal, Samuel, but it's because you are a man grown, and in some ways Anna is still innocent."

Anna felt her face flame. She stared at her lap,

rolling the hem of her apron into a tight ball. Was Aunt Jezebel really making a reference to what went on between a man and a wife in the privacy of their bedroom?

"Where you are used to living a married life," Aunt Jezebel continued, "our Anna is a good girl. We trust her."

"I'd never do anything to harm Anna or shame her, Jezebel. You need to know that about me."

Aunt Jezebel's pale blue eyes took on a piercing expression that Anna had never seen before. "I can see you'd never *intentionally* do anything to hurt our Anna, but we know that you are human, as are we all. We are frail, sometimes weak. And the call of the flesh can be strong."

Samuel nodded. "That's true enough, I suppose."

"Sanctioned by marriage, physical love is a beautiful thing," Aunt Jezebel continued, "or so the preachers tell me. I never married myself. It wasn't God's plan for me. But Anna's mother and her family would not be doing their job to protect her if they—if *we* weren't careful."

"I understand," Samuel said. "But like I said, you have nothing to worry about in me. I've nothing but honorable intentions concerning Anna."

"Good. Glad we've got that said between us." Aunt Jezebel hit the table lightly three times with the palm of her hand, and then motioned to Anna. "Now fetch Samuel another piece of pie and refill his coffee cup. He has a cold drive home, and he'll need to fortify himself."

"No need," Samuel said, rising. "As you say, it's late. I should go."

Anna walked to the porch with him. "You mustn't mind Aunt Jezebel," she said softly, so Aunt Jezebel couldn't hear her. "She's old-fashioned and—"

"She was fine," Samuel said. "She was just trying to make it clear that your family cares about you and wants what's best for you. I didn't mind." He smiled at her. "Even if I did hope to steal a kiss tonight."

Anna took a step back and pulled her father's old coat closer around her shoulders. "You'll get no kisses from me until we're joined in marriage— if we are. I'm still not at peace in my heart about this, Samuel. I'm honored by your asking, but…"

"Did you have fun tonight?"

"In spite of everything?" she asked, glancing back over her shoulder at the kitchen. "Even after this *talk* with Aunt Jezebel?" She dared a little smile. "I did."

"Good. Then that's where we'll leave it for now. Don't let me rush you into a decision you're not sure of. Stand your ground, Anna. I like it when you do."

"All right," she promised.

"You'll still be able to watch the children on Friday for me?"

"*Ya*. I will. Count on it. I'll come over early." She hesitated. "Will you think about taking Naomi with you?"

He smiled and shrugged. "Once you get a thing in your head, you're as stubborn as your mother. I'll think about it."

She offered him a shy smile, went back into the kitchen and closed the door firmly behind her. Inside, she found that Aunt Jezebel had already gone to bed, so she blew out the lamp and made her way up the staircase to her bedroom. The truth was, she wanted Samuel Mast for her husband. She wanted him more than anything in the world...but she still wasn't convinced that she deserved him.

Chapter Twelve

On Friday morning, Anna, Leah and Grossmama arrived at Samuel's at 7:00 a.m., just as Samuel was preparing to get into a gray van driven by an Englisher who Anna recognized. "Morning, Samuel," she called. "Morning, Rodger."

Leah reined in the horse and Samuel turned to smile at them. "You're here bright and early."

Anna saw that there were other Amish already in the van, three men and two women. Only one was a member of their church, but she knew them all, and she waved to them as well. "Told you we would be here early," Anna replied. *How fine Samuel looks,* she thought with a little thrill. Properly Plain, of course, but well dressed in solid boots, a new wool hat and a heavy coat. He looked like what he was—a solid and prosperous farmer.

Samuel walked over to the buggy. "The boys are finishing up morning chores, but the little ones are still abed. Mae had us up three times last night, with those bad dreams of hers. Screaming fit to bring the roof down. And when you wake her, she just cries and cries. Hope she's not a handful for you today."

"You go enjoy the auction," Anna assured him. "I'll look after the children."

"Don't let them burn down the house," he cautioned.

Leah chuckled. "We won't."

Samuel returned to the van, opened its sliding door, raised his thumb and forefinger to his mouth and whistled.

Naomi came flying out of the house and down the walk, boots untied, her best black bonnet in one hand and a book in the other. "Don't leave without me! I'm coming, Dat!"

"Put on your bonnet, girl," Samuel said. "What are you thinking?" She did as he bid her, and he straightened the bonnet over her white *kapp,* and tied the strings firmly under her chin. "Now, into the van. Hurry." He tempered his firm words with a grin. "Driver won't wait all day."

"So you decided to take Naomi after all?" Anna tried to suppress her satisfaction that Samuel had listened to her. "I'm so glad."

"Told you I'd think on it," he said. "Spoke to Joe, heard some other womenfolk would be there, so I thought, why not? It's a small thing to do, if it pleases you. Why not?"

"And Naomi," she reminded him. "Your daughter most of all. It's not a small matter to her." From her seat by the window, Naomi sat up tall and smiled shyly.

Leah waved and Naomi returned the wave.

"Have a good time," Anna called.

"Can't say what time this will be over," Samuel said, still looking at Anna.

"Don't worry. A hot supper will be waiting when you get here."

"Make sure the boys get to school on time."

The driver leaned toward Samuel and said something that Anna couldn't make out, and Samuel closed the sliding door and got into the front passenger seat. As the engine started, he rolled down the window and called, "I told Peter and Rudy that if there's trouble, I'll know the reason why."

"Go!" Anna said, laughing. *Men.* To make such a fuss over being away from the farm for a day. As if she couldn't manage four children. As mischievous as boys could be, compared to Grossmama, dealing with Samuel's twins was a piece of cake.

By the time Lori Ann and Mae woke and wandered down to the kitchen in their long nightgowns, Anna had apple pancakes and sausage cooking on the big gas stove, and Leah was topping mugs of hot chocolate with tiny marshmallows. Lori Ann rubbed her eyes and said, "Our dat—dat's g-g-gone away and you c-c-came to t-t-t-take care of us." Mae only stared and popped her thumb into her mouth.

"Indeed we have," Anna said. She noticed that Mae's feet were bare. Sweeping her up, she hugged her and wrapped her in a furry throw that was hanging near the cupboard, and plopped her down into Grossmama's arms. One looked as surprised as the other, but her grandmother nodded and began to rock the child and sing a lullaby to her in the old dialect.

"Mae had a—a—a b-bad dream l-l-last night," Lori Ann said. "And—and she wet her night— nightgown."

Mae hid her face in Grossmama's large bosom, but her stiff little body softened as she cuddled against the old woman. Grossmama stroked the child's back and whispered in her ear, "It's all right. Just a dream."

Anna glanced at Leah, who shrugged. Whatever the reason, Anna was glad that her grandmother had obviously taken to Mae and the little girl to her.

Anna wiped her hands on a towel and crouched down beside them. "This gown?" she asked, sniffing the material and feeling it. It felt dry, and all she could smell was the sweet scent of a clean child.

Lori Ann shook her head. "*Ne.* Naomi…she gave

her a—a—a b-b-b-bath and put a-a-another night-gown on her."

Anna pursed her lips and sighed. "She's a good sister, Naomi. She takes care of her like a little mother."

"Me t-t-too," Lori Ann ventured. "I—I—I'm a—a—a g-good g-g-girl."

"Ya," Anna agreed, giving the child an approving glance. "You are a very good girl, to always think about your little sister." Lori Ann straightened her shoulders and smiled. "The best," Anna said.

She was so glad that Naomi had gotten to go with Samuel today. It wasn't fair that she spend her entire childhood taking care of a house and her younger siblings. Again came the thought that Samuel really needed a mother for the five of them. Providing a home and working a farm was work enough for any man, without having to do it all alone. Maybe this was God's wish for Anna, that she care for these children, even if there would be no love in the marriage. How was she supposed to know?

"Now, you go and eat your breakfast like a good girl, Martha." Grossmama stood Mae on her feet. "And someone find some stockings and shoes for this baby before she catches the ague."

"Can you show me where her things are?" Leah

asked Lori Ann. The girl nodded and the two hurried off.

Anna lifted Mae into a plastic booster seat on a chair, and slid her up to the table. Anna took a sip of the hot chocolate to see that it wasn't too hot, and then handed the cup to the child. She glanced at the clock, then went to the kitchen door, opened it and struck the iron triangle to call the boys to breakfast. Soon Rudy and Peter came charging in, Leah and Lori Ann returned with the thick stockings for Mae, and everyone, including Grossmama, gathered around the big table for breakfast.

"Look at those hands," Grossmama snapped at Rudy. "You do not eat with hands like those. To the sink, both of you." Her order encompassed a grinning Peter. "Soap. Scrub hard. You need clean hands for school." The twins went without argument, and the rest of the meal passed by without a hitch.

Anna was glad she'd offered to bring Grossmama over early with her, rather than picking her up on the way to Byler's store. Mam had looked doubtful when she'd suggested it, but Aunt Jezebel had clearly been pleased to get a few hours' respite from her sister's constant complaints. And Leah had cheerfully offered to help out Anna for the day. Instead of a problem, Grossmama had turned out to be a blessing.

Getting her grandmother up and dressed in time

to get Samuel's children off to school hadn't been difficult, because Lovina had gotten up before daylight every day of her life, and saw no reason to change her routine at this age. "This is a good house," Grossmama said, after the boys left for school, leaving only the women and girls to clean up the kitchen. She waved a hand, taking in the spacious kitchen, the oak cupboards and the sturdy table that sat twelve. "I've always liked this house."

"You've never been to Samuel's before, have you?" Leah asked.

"Snickerdoodles," Grossmama snapped. "We moved here back in the spring of…well, I don't rec- ollect the year exactly. Sometimes my mind plays tricks on me. But two of my girls were born here— and my Jonas. He was the best baby, if I do say so. Not colicky like Martha here." She indicated Mae, who returned the attention with a lopsided smile. "A fine, healthy baby, my Jonas. A little wood- chopper to help his father."

Leah looked at Anna, and Anna shook her head. If Grossmama was satisfied, what good would it do to upset her by correcting her? Mae didn't seem to care that Lovina called her Martha, and Anna doubted there was much chance of winning the argument that this was Samuel's house and not Grossmama's.

"So," Anna said, when the girls were dressed, the kitchen was shining and a pot of dried butter beans were soaking in a pot on the back of the stove. "Who wants to go to Byler's?"

"Me!" Lori Ann cried. Mae nodded.

Anna smiled at them. They looked so cute in their starched white *kapps* and cornflower-blue dresses that Samuel's sister, Louise, had sewn and sent from Ohio. Anna knew it was as hard for Louise to be separated from little Mae as it was for the child to be apart from the only mother she'd even known, but Louise had a big family of her own. Sending Mae back to Samuel had been a difficult choice, but the right thing to do. When a child had a loving father, she should be with him, not only for their sakes but for Naomi, Lori Ann and the boys.

Mae's return had shaken up the household in more ways than one. Lori Ann, who was naturally shy and had a speech problem, was no longer the baby; and Naomi, who was already overworked, had even more to do. Anna's heart went out to these motherless children. If only she knew for certain that there was the possibility that Samuel could learn to love her, despite her size and lack of looks, she would have been thrilled to take on that challenge.

The back door banged open and Rudy dashed back in. "Where's our lunch?" he asked.

Anna looked at Leah. Leah grimaced. "I guess we forgot," she admitted.

"Naomi is supposed to make our lunch," Rudy said, rocking from one snowy boot to the other. He stood with the door still half open behind him.

"Shut that door," Grossmama ordered. "Were you born in a barn, Jonas?"

"I'm Rudy," he said, but he meekly pushed the door shut.

"I know who you are," Grossmama said. "You're trying to trick me, pretending there's two of you, but I know better. You're my Jonas. But if you were Bishop Ash, I'd still tell you to shut that door and not let the heat out!"

Anna scanned Samuel's spacious kitchen. On wrought iron hooks near the door, three black lunch kettles hung. She opened one after another, but all were empty. "You go on to school," she said to Rudy. "I'll make you each a lunch and drop it off in the cloak room as we go out to Byler's."

"I want bologna," Rudy said. "Two slices with cheese in the middle, and catsup on my bread. Potato chips. And cookies—six."

"You'll eat what we give you," Grossmama said, "And be glad to get it. When I was a girl, my Mam gave us boiled squirrels, still with the head and bones, and corn bread in our lunch pails and we were glad to get it. A bear killed our hogs, and all the meat we had one winter was wild game my father shot." She made a shooing motion. "Go on. You heard my Anna. Off to school with you, Jonas."

Rudy stiffened. He started to say something, then eyed Grossmama warily, thought the better of it, and ducked back out onto the porch. Anna followed him.

"Don't worry," she promised. "I'll give you plenty to eat."

He spun around suddenly. "You aren't our Mam, you know," he said in a mean voice. "And we don't like you. You're fat and ugly and Dat won't ever marry you."

Anna gasped. Hurt tightened her throat. "That's a rude thing to say, Rudy. Your father would be ashamed of you."

"We don't need you. We don't need anybody. This is our house, and we don't want you here." He turned and looked at his twin, who was standing on the sidewalk a few yards from the house. "Do we, Peter? Tell her. We don't want her here."

Peter put his fingers in the corners of his mouth, stretched his mouth wide and stuck out his tongue. "Fatty, fatty, two-by-four!" he shouted. "Can't get through the kitchen door!" And before Anna could gather her wits and think of a suitable comeback, both boys ran, leaving her standing, eyes stinging with tears, on the cold, windy back porch.

Even on a cold Friday morning in January, Byler's was bustling with Amish, Mennonites, local Englishers and a scattering of tourists with their outlandish dress and out-of-state license plates on their big fancy cars. Anna felt more at home at Byler's than she did in the Dover supermarkets or Walmarts. The Kent County folk had lived with their Plain neighbors for generations, and few stared and pointed as the strangers did.

Sometimes tourists tried to sneak pictures of the Amish. It was rude and embarrassing. Photographs were against the Ordnung. Anna had been baptized into the church when she was fifteen, and she'd never willingly permitted her snapshot to be taken. But sometimes Englishers jumped out, a flash went off in her face, and then what could she do?

Leah never seemed to get upset by the intrusions. "They don't know any better," she said. "We're lucky that no one wanders into the house like the Englishers do in Lancaster. Pauline's sister tells her that they have tourists walking in all the time. There is a sign on the far side of their property, pointing to the 'Old Amish Farm,' and people mistake their house for the showplace."

"I don't know why anyone would want to see our house anyway," Anna said. "I don't go into their homes and stare."

Leah chuckled. "Because Mam taught us better."

Anna was still smarting over the way Rudy and Peter had acted. Their cruel words hurt, but a secret voice whispered that they were right. Samuel would never marry her, and if he did he might be sorry.

Leah and Anna each took a cart and put the girls in the seats, so that they wouldn't have to chase them. "C-c-can we have i-i-ice c-cream?" Lori Ann whispered. "I l-l-l-like i-i-ice c-cream."

"You certainly can," Anna promised. "But only if you are very good."

Grossmama took a cart, as well. Anna had offered to push her in a wheelchair, but her grandmother had scoffed at riding in a moving chair. "They have motors," she confided, "like cars. They run away with you." So Grossmama pushed her own cart and happily loaded it with cinnamon, nutmeg, walnuts and oatmeal.

"That's too much," Leah murmured in Anna's ear, but Anna only smiled. "We'll put some back later. Let her please herself. She seems to be having such a good time. And she'll get tired."

Byler's store had begun on the back porch of a local farmhouse, when the founder had started going to the city to buy staples in large amounts for his big family. Like a weed patch, it had grown and grown, until it was now a large, modern business that specialized in discount groceries. The inventory included wood stoves and a wide array of kitchen items, as well as a produce and dairy section, a bakery and a deli. Best of all, Byler's sold fresh-dipped ice-cream cones at a very reasonable price.

Soon, as Anna had guessed, Lovina's steps grew

slower. "I'm tired," she said. "And I'm hungry. I want a submarine sandwich."

"And—and we want i-i-ice c-cream," Lori Ann reminded.

"I know just the place for you to eat your lunch," Anna said. She guided the family back to the entrance lobby, where the store workers had placed long wooden picnic tables. She found a seat for Grossmama next to two elderly Mennonite ladies, gave her the oversized sandwich, napkins and her orange soda pop. "We'll be glad to sit here with you, if you want," Anna offered.

"Ne, ne." Grossmama beamed, and Anna could tell that she was delighted to be sitting where she could stare to her heart's delight at all the folks coming and going.

Leah looked dubious. "You won't wander off, will you? Remember what happened when we took you to the hardware store in Ohio? You took the buggy and—"

"You hush that talk," Grossmama said. "Jonas took me home. You never mind that. I want to eat my lunch in quiet. You two finish your shopping and buy those children their ice cream."

"Don't want ice-cream cone," Mae said, stretching out her arms to Grossmama. "Want to stay *wiff* her."

"You need to come with me, honey," Anna said gently. "Grossmama wants to eat her lunch."

"Ne!" Mae stuck out her lip. "Stay *wiff* her!"

"Give the child here," Grossmama said, scooting over on the picnic bench. "Martha can help me eat my submarine. She can sit right here."

Anna looked at Leah. Their gazes locked and Leah nodded. "That will be fine," she said, lifting Mae out of her cart.

"But if…" Anna began.

Leah smiled. "Grossmama will take good care of her," she said.

"Stop your chattering, you two. Finish your shopping and let us eat," Lovina said. Mae climbed up on the bench beside her, and Grossmama tore off a piece of sandwich and handed it to the child.

Leah motioned to the sliding door that led back inside the main shopping area. "She'll be fine. Grossmama is always better when she has something to do."

Behind them, Anna heard a woman remark in a New York accent, "Look at that adorable little *Aim-ish* girl in the bonnet. Isn't she precious? Take our picture, Phil. I'm sure they won't mind."

"No pictures!" Grossmama said. "You should be ashamed of yourself! Didn't your mother teach you better? And why are you coming to Byler's in your undershift?"

Inside, Anna turned back to intervene, only to see Grossmama had pulled Mae into her lap. Mae hid her face against Lovina, and Grossmama had thrown her shawl over the girl's head. The two Mennonite women were laughing, and the Englisher lady in a very short skirt began to sputter. Before she could do more than utter a squeak, the man with her had grabbed her arm and pulled her back outside. Grossmama had picked up her sub and continued eating as though nothing had happened.

Leah dissolved into laughter. She and Anna laughed until tears ran down their faces, and Lori Ann was giggling, too. Finally, when Leah could speak again, she said, "You go on and finish the shopping. I was planning on standing here and watching them. Grossmama can't see me, but I can be sure she or Mae don't come to harm."

"You don't mind?"

"*Ne.* Rebecca and I did it all the time. It hurts her feelings if she thinks you are treating her like a child."

"I…want my ice-cream c-cone," Lori Ann said. "I was g-good, Anna."

"*Ya,* very good," Anna agreed. Still smiling, she pushed the grocery cart away toward the ice-cream counter. "What kind shall we get?"

"Make mine butter pecan," Leah called after them. "Two scoops."

The rest of the day went as smooth for Anna as cake flour sliding through her fingers. Leah drove the horse and buggy from Byler's to the Yoder home without a mishap. Rebecca and Susanna came out to help unload their purchases, and Aunt Jezebel helped Grossmama into the house. She was tired and wanted her afternoon nap. Mae was sleepy, as well, and fell asleep in Anna's arms, somewhere between Mam's house and Samuel's. She didn't wake when Anna laid her on the daybed in the kitchen, and covered her up with a soft throw.

"I—I have to g-gather the—the eggs," Lori Ann said. "It's my job."

Anna glanced at the time. Soon the boys would be home from school, and she wanted to get a start on supper. She hadn't had a minute alone with Leah, to tell her about the twins' bad behavior this morning, and she was still stinging from their taunts. She didn't doubt that she could manage these little girls if she and Samuel were to marry, but what if it was different with Rudy and Peter? What if they really didn't like her? Would it drive a wedge between Samuel and his sons?

She closed her eyes, said a quick but fervent prayer for guidance, and did what she did best— cooked. By the time Samuel and Naomi came in at 6:30, the kitchen smelled of hot biscuits, fried ham, hot applesauce and butter beans and dumplings.

Samuel walked past her, opened the oven door and grinned when he saw the bread pudding bubbling inside. "Anna, Anna," he said in his big, deep voice. "You are wonderful. Here I am, thinking it was cold ham sandwiches and canned soup for us, and you've cooked up a feast." Lori Ann ran to her father, and he popped a piece of biscuit into her mouth, picked her up and lifted her high in the air before giving her a hug.

Satisfaction filled Anna with a delicious warmth. "And how was the auction?" She didn't need to ask if Naomi had a good time. The girl's shining face told it all. "Good. Good," Samuel said, grabbing a hot biscuit and tossing it from one big hand to another before taking a bite. "How was your day? You make out okay? Looks like you did. I haven't seen the kitchen this clean in ages."

"We had a fine day, we girls." She had no intention of telling Samuel about the twins' rudeness. She'd decided that the boys were her problem to solve. "But I'd rather hear about the auction, than talk of shopping and cooking."

"Wait until you see what I bought."

"What is it?" Anna asked.

"I'm not telling," he replied. "You'll see soon enough. It's a surprise."

"Oh, a surprise?" Anna found herself truly curious.

"You'll see next week," he said with a grin. "And by the way, the weatherman is calling for eight inches of snow next week."

Chapter Thirteen

The following day, Anna rose early to start the fire in the wood-burning cook stove, to make morning biscuits, and found Grossmama already at the table drinking coffee. After greeting Lovina, Anna went to the gas stove, picked up the coffeepot and poured herself a cup. To her surprise, the coffee was excellent. "Did you make this?" she asked her grandmother.

Grossmama laughed and shook her head. "Jezzy doesn't let me use the gas stove. Thinks I'm not right in the head. She made the coffee."

At the mention of her name, Aunt Jezebel came into the kitchen from the hallway, fully dressed but with her damp hair wrapped in a towel. "We got up first. First up makes the coffee," her aunt explained.

"There!" Grossmama slapped a color brochure on the table. "I want you to see this." She looked at Anna. "See." She tapped the paper.

Anna picked up the brochure and examined it. The cover read "Maple Leaf Center. Join active seniors in your community for crafts, fellowship and education. Monday through Friday. Luncheon and transportation provided." Pictured was a one-story brick building with a red metal roof and window boxes full of flowers.

Puzzled, Anna glanced at Grossmama. "This is a place for older people to gather and visit?"

"Read it," Lovina said impatiently.

Anna unfolded the colorful brochure and looked at the photos of a library, a dining room with smiling English people sitting at round tables, a table where two women were sitting and knitting and a line of people climbing into a large sightseeing bus.

"And on the back," Grossmama insisted. "There's more on the back."

The last picture was of a group of women sitting around a quilting stand piecing together a quilt. But one woman was braiding strips of cloth. In her lap lay the beginnings of a braided rug.

"They make rugs," Grandmother said. "I want to go there. I want to ride in the red van. I make the best rugs. I can show those English women what they are doing wrong."

"I tried to tell her that this Maple Leaf place was for Englishers," Aunt Jezzy said, "but…" She spread her palms in a hopeless gesture.

"I want to go," Grossmama repeated. "I want to go tomorrow. Today, I want to go home to my house. Jonas left the door open. The kitchen will get cold."

"I tried to tell her that was Samuel's house she's thinking of, and Samuel's boy," her aunt said. "But she never listens to me."

Mam and Susanna walked into the kitchen. "Leah and Rebecca are still sleeping," Anna's mother said. "Not that I blame them on such a cold, bleak day."

"It's going to snow," Grossmama announced. "I can always smell snow." She glared at Hannah. "I'm going home before it snows. Tell that Irwin boy to hitch up the horse."

"You're right about the snow, Lovina," Hannah said. "I turned on Jonas's radio to listen to the weather, and there was an announcement. Church will be canceled this Sunday if we get more than four inches." She smiled at Grossmama. "I hope you enjoyed your trip to Byler's yesterday."

"Martha and I had a submarine sandwich and we saw an Englisher woman in her shift."

"What?" Mam asked.

"I'll explain later," Anna promised.

"I'm going to ride in the red van," Grossmama went on. "And you can't stop me. I'm going to make braided rugs, hundreds of them. I make the best."

"Sister, let's get you dressed while Hannah and

the girls make breakfast," Aunt Jezebel said, taking Lovina's arm.

"I want eggs." Grossmama pointed at Anna. "And you make them. Hannah is a terrible cook. Her eggs taste like cow pies." She narrowed her eyes and peered around the room. "She's a thief, too. She sneaks into my room at night and takes my pocketbook."

"Mam would never do such a thing," Anna defended.

"Would too!" Grossmama said. "I had thirty-five dollars and now I have twenty-six dollars and fifteen cents."

"You bought a submarine sandwich and mints yesterday," Aunt Jezebel reminded her. "Hannah would never steal from you."

"So you say." Grossmama shuffled across the kitchen. "You're probably in it together, taking my money while I'm asleep."

"That's not very kind of you, Lovina. And it's not kind of you to speak of Hannah's cooking that way, either."

Grossmama thrust out her lower lip, but said no more.

"Anna will make your eggs just the way you like them," Hannah promised.

"How do you stand it?" Anna asked, when her grandmother and aunt had gone back to their bedroom. "She's not mean to me. You should have seen her yesterday. She was so good with Samuel's Mae, and the child adores her."

"Pray for her, Anna," her mother said with a sigh. "She's confused and far from home. She's lost her husband, her only son, her brothers and two of her daughters. And thank the Good Lord that you weren't born with Lovina's disposition. I do, every day."

By eleven o'clock that morning, heavy snow began to fall, large lacy flakes that tumbled and piled on the windowsills, and gathered in drifts around the porch. Anna and her sisters helped Irwin stable all the livestock in the barn, heaping their stalls high with bright straw and filling their water pails. It was cold, but not the usual bitter cold that came with heavy snowfalls in Delaware. And the wind, surprisingly, held little force; and the farm took on a wintery, white beauty, as snow covered the roofs and lawn and barnyard.

Anna kept busy, first with the outside chores and then in the house. Everyone was glad to gather around the table for a hearty dinner of beef stew and apple fritters. Grossmama continued to insist that she was going to Maple Leaf Center and to argue that she needed to go home before the storm got any worse. Mam had given all of them a look that told them to keep a sharp eye on their grandmother. They couldn't have her wandering out of the house in the middle of a snowstorm.

But in spite of all she did with her hands, Anna's mind remained on Samuel and his children. She wondered how were they faring today. Had Samuel had time to prepare them a hot meal? Was Naomi able to manage both small sisters and still work her way through the inside chores? And then there were the tougher questions. Did Samuel really care for her, or was she—Anna—a poor substitute for the beautiful wife he'd loved and lost? And what was she going to do about the twins? Provided, of course, that she decided that she wanted Samuel to court her. She had to make up her mind about him before she could solve the other problems.

"Where's your husband, Anna?" Grossmama asked.

It was late in the afternoon. Mam and the girls were cleaning the upstairs, and Anna was just finishing up in the kitchen. It was still snowing, and Anna had paused, a dishcloth in her hand, to stare out the window. She'd thought Grossmama was napping. Obviously, not. "I don't have a husband," she said. "I'm not married."

"Well, don't wait too long. A big girl like you. Strong and sweet. You'll make some man a good wife, Anna. Don't be too fussy, like Jezzy. You wait too long, you'll wither on the vine."

She turned toward her grandmother. "You think I'd make a good wife?" So what if Grossmama's memory failed her and she was sometimes confused? It would make Anna feel better to hear someone besides her mother say so. "You don't think I'm too...too Plain?"

"Too Plain to be a wife? No such thing! Potatoes. I like potatoes. I don't like rice." Then Grossmama paused, as if deep in thought. "My nose was too long. I was too tall and skinny. Didn't make a bit of difference to Jonas's dat. He wasn't all that much to look at either."

Anna nibbled on her lower lip. How could her grandmother be so sensible one moment, and then so confused the next? As prickly as the old woman was, Anna still loved her and wished she could find some way to ease the tensions between Grossmama and Mam.

Lovina hobbled to the window, leaned on her cane and stared out. "Hope my geese are snug in their shed." She glanced at Anna. "You need your own flock, girl, for when you marry. Every wife needs poultry. Whatever money comes from the ducks and geese and chickens, that's hers by right. Not the husband's. A woman needs her own money." She sniffed. "Especially in this house, where they're all trying to steal every penny I've got."

"You worry a lot about money, Grossmama,"

Anna said, touching her grandmother's arm. "You don't have to. We'll take care of you. We want to take care of you."

"Got to worry about money. Never enough. We lived on squirrels one winter when I was a girl. Did I tell you that?"

Anna nodded. "You did. Was that when you lived in the Kishacoquillas Valley?"

Lovina snorted. "Valley, nothing. We lived on the mountain. My dat was too poor to own bottom-land. Rock and trees, that's what he tilled, rock and trees. Bears and wild things eating our livestock, and him with eighteen mouths to fill. I was the oldest girl. Many a day, I'd give my dinner to the little ones and go without. Never enough money. Got to get yourself a flock of geese, Anna. If you've got poultry, you'll always have a full purse."

Anna wrapped her big hand around her grandmother's bony one and tried to imagine a tall, skinny girl in a *kapp* going hungry to feed her younger brothers and sisters. She looked around Mam's kitchen and thought how fortunate she'd been to be born here in Kent County, where there were no bears to steal the winter's meat and no rocks to litter the fertile fields. Other than fasting days, Anna couldn't ever remember going hungry, and her heart went out to her brave and tough grandmother.

"I'll remember that, Grossmama," she said. "And

when spring comes, I promise I'll buy some baby goslings and start my own flock."

"I'll show you how to collect the down," Grossmama said. "But your Samuel can't have the money. It's yours, and that's all there is to it."

"He isn't my Samuel," Anna said softly.

Lovina snorted again. "Of course he is. He's your husband, isn't he? And a fine man, too, to give you all those beautiful children."

"They are beautiful, but Rudy and Peter don't like me," Anna admitted. "They don't want me to marry their father."

"Not up to children," her grandmother said. "Up to the Lord. He decides."

"You really believe that?" She stroked Lovina's hand. "That God has a plan for each of us, even for me?"

"'Course He has a plan. For all of us. He wants me to go to that Maple Leaf in the red van. I'm going tomorrow, right after I go home to Martha and Jonas."

There was no church service on Sunday. Out on the main roads, the big snowplows roared, but few cars and trucks passed the farm. By midmorning, the snowfall had trickled to tiny flakes, glittering like stars in the sunshine. Charley and Eli came up to the big house and got Irwin, and the three of them shoveled paths to the barn, chicken house and pigpen. They threw bales of hay down from the loft, and broke the ice in the water troughs, to see that all the animals had plenty to drink.

Anna was just sweeping snow off the porch when she heard the sound of bells and looked up to see Samuel's Morgan horse come around the barn, pulling a beautiful, old-fashioned sleigh. Anna's eyes widened in astonishment. "Samuel," she called to him. "Whatever are you driving?"

"Do you like it?" he asked. "This is the surprise I told you about." He reined in Smoky, and Anna saw Mae's small face peering out from a mound of blankets in her father's lap.

Excitement made Anna giddy. The beautiful horse, the black-and-gold sleigh that looked like something out of a storybook, took her breath away. "You bought a sleigh," she said. "I…I love it."

"The man I bought it from said he had it for years, mostly collecting dust in his shed." He grinned and offered his hand. "Climb up, Anna. I came to take you for a sleigh ride."

"Me?"

His laughter rang out across the yard. "What other Anna could I be asking to ride with me on such a beautiful Sunday?"

"I…" She wanted to go. She'd never wanted anything so badly than to ride in that shining sleigh with Samuel behind a high-stepping horse. Samuel could have asked any of a dozen young women. He could have asked her sister, Leah, but he'd asked *her.*

"I...I'll have to ask my mother," she said.

"Ne." His smile lit up his whole face and his beautiful eyes sparkled. "Decide for yourself, Anna. You're a woman, full grown. Church has been cancelled, so that makes this a visiting Sunday. Come visit with me. I mean to check in on the old and sick, to be certain they have all they need." He offered his hand again. "Come away with me, Anna Yoder. Or stand here and wish you had," he teased, pulling away his hand. "Who knows when there will be another snow like this?"

Anna took a deep breath and glanced at Charley, who was still digging a space around the chicken house door. "Should I go?" she asked.

"Ne," Samuel said again. "You must decide, Anna. Are we courting or not?"

"Courting is not a promise of marriage," she answered.

"But few marriages go forward without it."

She looked back toward the house and saw Aunt Jezebel's pale face staring out. If she didn't take this chance, she might end up like her aunt, and she didn't want that.

"All right," she said, and put her hand into his. To her surprise, he leaped down out of the sleigh and helped her to climb in. She was afraid that her weight would be too much for him, but he lifted her in his strong arms, as though she were no bigger than Miriam. In two flicks of Smoky's tail, she was sitting in the deep seat, her legs and shoulders swathed in blankets.

Samuel climbed back up, picked up the leathers and shook them over the Morgan's back. With a jingle of bells, they were off across the barnyard, down the orchard lane and across the field, toward her Aunt Martha's house. Snow flew from the horse's hooves and the harness creaked. Snowflakes swirled through the air and landed on Anna's face.

Beside her, little Mae giggled and opened her mouth. "Taste good," she said.

"Do they?" Anna asked. She tilted her head back and mimicked the child. And soon Samuel was doing the same. Laughing, they bounced and slid over the deep snow, and Anna marveled at how fast they covered the distance. Eventually, Mae wiggled off her father's lap and into Anna's. She was warm and soft, and Anna felt a surge of love fill her. Maybe her grandmother was right, she thought. Maybe God did have a plan for her. And maybe, if she was lucky, Samuel would be part of it.

He leaned close. "So you admit that I'm courting you? That if we suit each other you'd be willing to become my wife?"

"I'm thinking on it."

Samuel laughed again, and the sound of his big, booming voice was like music to her ears. "You are a stubborn woman," he pronounced.

"Ne," she answered. "My Aunt Martha is a stubborn woman. Something tells me that she won't be happy to see us together."

Samuel nodded. "You're right, but who better to let know our secret. By tomorrow morning, snowstorm or no snowstorm, every family in the county will know that we're walking out together." Snowflakes lodged in his beard, and Anna reached up and brushed them away.

"Was that so hard?" he asked, looking into her eyes.

"What?" She was suddenly shy. This wasn't happening to her, couldn't be. What had she done to deserve such a beau?

"To touch me, Anna? To smile at me? You don't know how many nights I've lain awake wondering what was wrong with me, wondering why you didn't want me." He draped a big arm around her shoulders and pulled her and Mae closer to him. "I love you, Anna. You may not believe it, but I do." He leaned even closer, and before she knew it, Samuel's lips brushed hers.

Anna's heart skipped and hammered against her ribs. For long seconds the snowy landscape, the sled, the horse, everything, vanished. There was nothing but the sweet sensation of Samuel's kiss. And then she realized where she was and what she'd just permitted. She pulled away just as horse and sleigh broke out of the woods' lane and into Aunt Martha's yard.

Dorcas, carrying two buckets of water to the barn, stopped gape-mouthed and stared, so surprised that she dropped her buckets. "Anna?"

Aunt Martha came out of the chicken house with a basket of eggs. She wore a denim coat of Uncle Reuben's, men's high rubber boots and a blue wool scarf over her head. "Whatever are you doing in that contraption?" Aunt Martha cried. "On a Sabbath. With Samuel Mast?" she demanded. "Reuben! Reuben! Come see this."

"Good day, Martha, Dorcas," Samuel called, merrily. "Just checking to see that you have everything you need. What with the snow and the roads blocked."

"You have Anna alone in that sleigh? With bells?"

Samuel shook his head. "The bells are on Smoky, Martha. No bells on Anna. Her mother wouldn't approve."

Anna saw Dorcas standing behind her mother, break into a grin.

"Don't worry. We have Mae with us."

Her aunt huffed. "A child? Hardly a proper chaperone." She glanced around and shouted again. "Reuben!"

"Certain you have everything you need?" Samuel asked.

"This is not right. Not proper," Aunt Martha declared.

"Then we'll be off," Samuel called with a wave. "Lots of families to visit."

"See you at church next week," Anna called, mischievously. And then they were off again, flying over the ground, charging through the snowy fields on a thrilling and heart-pounding ride.

Chapter Fourteen

The snow didn't last. The following week, a warm front moved across the state, and heavy rains washed away the accumulation of snow. Samuel's beautiful sleigh was stored in his carriage shed, covered with a tarp, to wait for another day when travel by buggy was impossible. Anna's ride with Samuel had caused quite a flutter in the community, but her mother and sisters were more than ready to support her.

"I told Lydia that Samuel couldn't find a better wife if he searched every Amish community in the county," Mam told Ruth one afternoon.

Ruth's Eli had been working late at the chair shop, so she'd walked across the field to visit with the family. She'd brought Grossmama some lovely strips of blue wool for the rug she was working on.

It was Thursday, and Mam had a school board meeting at seven, at Roman's house, so they'd planned an early supper. "It's time Anna had a little fun. Who deserves it more?"

Anna busied herself at the sink, carefully washing the battered copper pot that Grossmama had brought with her from Ohio. The pot, called a kettle, had been purchased in Philadelphia as a gift for a bride, long before Pennsylvania became one of the original thirteen colonies. It was her grandmother's most cherished possession, handed down through the family for generations.

"That kettle goes to Anna when I die," Grossmama said. "Martha will kick up a fuss, but she's not to have it. Martha couldn't make peach jam without burning it, to save her soul, and she doesn't deserve it."

"Now, sister," Aunt Jezebel interjected. "You're too hard on Martha."

"Martha's too hard on me. Like to killed me, getting born. I was in labor with her for three days. It's a wonder either of us lived." Lovina was seated in the big rocking chair near the stove, where she'd supervised the making of a batch of apple butter. "Is the van here yet? I'm waiting for the van to take me to the center."

Grossmama had been asking all day about the van that would take her to Maple Leaf.

"Couldn't we arrange for her to go to the center just once?" Anna quietly asked her mother, when

Hannah had brought her a clean towel to dry the kettle. "She seems set on going."

Mam sighed. "Maple Leaf is for the English. Plain People don't go there. We provide for our older family members in our homes. We don't need the help of strangers to do what's right."

"But what harm could it do if she wants to go?" Anna persisted.

Her mother shook her head. "Bishop Atlee wouldn't allow it. It wouldn't look right."

Ruth joined them. "We are a people apart from the world, Anna."

"But why is it wrong for Grossmama to spend time with the English, if it would be good for her?"

"We must live by the Ordnung," her mother said. "Sometimes it's hard, but our faith has sustained us through trial and hardship. We can't question the ways that have kept us on God's path."

"But what if Bishop Atlee agreed?" Anna dried the kettle with the dishtowel. "If he approved, would you let her go?"

"He won't," Ruth said. "No Amish have ever gone to Maple Leaf. I know, because my friend Flo works there in the kitchen."

"Is it a nice place?" Anna asked. "Do the Englishers treat the older people kindly?"

"Ya." Ruth nodded. "Flo says that everyone there is nice. Sometimes she helps with serving the lunch and cleaning the craft room."

"I was thinking," Anna began, and Mam laughed.

"What?" Anna asked.

"You've obviously been thinking hard about a lot of things. Samuel included."

"Ah, Samuel," Ruth teased. "How long are you going to keep him dangling?"

"She told Samuel that she'd give him an answer by her birthday," Mam said.

Ruth looked unconvinced. "But you should know by now whether you want him or not."

Mam chuckled. "And you didn't keep poor Eli dangling?"

"That was different," Ruth said. "I had to be certain that he was committed to the faith. I knew how I felt about him, but I could never have married anyone who wasn't as dedicated as I was. And Anna doesn't have that concern. She and Samuel both joined the church years ago."

"I'm just not sure," Anna said. "I care for Samuel, but I don't know if we're right for each other. If it's really God's plan for us."

"Because of those kids?" Ruth asked. "They'd be a handful, especially the boys."

"*Ne.*" Anna shook her head. "It would be easy to love them all. I think I do already. It's Samuel that troubles me. And me." She shrugged. "Look at me. Do I look like I belong with Samuel Mast?"

Her mother folded her arms and looked stern. "See how it is, Ruth? Your sister doesn't see herself as we see her—as beautiful and kind and strong. And as long as she can't love herself, she's not ready to accept the love of a man."

Anna swallowed. "You don't understand. You're my family. I know you love me. But maybe that love blinds you to who I really am?" Hanging her apron on the hook, she hurried out of the room and upstairs. Not even her mother or her sisters understood what it was like to be born ugly in a family of pretty faces. No one understood.

She hadn't even gotten to tell them about her idea for her grandmother. Next week, a truck would be bringing the rest of Aunt Jezzy and Grossmama's things. Her aunt had told her that Lovina had stacks of braided rugs that she'd made over the years. What Anna had thought was, that perhaps their sister Johanna could see if the English shops that sold her quilts would be interested in selling Grossmama's rugs. If they could sell some or all, Grossmama would have money of her own, and perhaps her mind would be at ease.

Upstairs in her room, Anna pulled her rocking chair to the window where she could catch the last of the daylight, and removed a new, pale green dress from her sewing basket. As she hemmed the dress, the tension seeped out of her shoulders and neck, and she began to softly hum an old hymn. She always felt better when her hands were busy and she felt useful.

The last time Naomi had been here, Anna had her try the dress on her, so it could be hemmed to the proper length. Samuel's sisters in Ohio kept the children in clothes, but the style wasn't always what the other children at school were wearing, and Naomi was at the age where she didn't want to look different. Anna could understand that perfectly. Surely, it wasn't vanity for Naomi to want her *kapps* and dresses to be like those of her friends. And Anna decided that she would ask Samuel when Naomi had last had her eyes checked. She spent a lot of time with her nose in a book, and it seemed to Anna that she was starting to squint. Maybe she needed a new prescription.

As Anna knotted the thread and put the last few stitches in the hem, Rudy's taunts rose in her mind, and again her stomach knotted. She would have to find a way to win over Samuel's twins, or there was no question of the two of them marrying. As Mam had said, she'd promised him an answer by her birthday, and that was only three weeks away. What if she was as undecided then as now? Would she have to refuse him? Better to say no than to say yes, and spend a lifetime doubting her choice.

"Anna?" Mam pushed open the bedroom door. "Are you sewing? Why didn't you light a lamp? You'll go blind."

She smiled at her mother. "*Ne*, Mam, I'll not go blind. You worry too much."

Mam came to sit on the edge of the bed near her. "I'm sorry if you felt pressured about Samuel. You know we all have your best interests at heart. We want you to be happy."

Anna smoothed the wrinkles from the small, neat dress. "You want me to marry him."

Mam shook her head. "Not if you don't want to."

Anna replaced her needle in its case, and tucked the spool of thread into the basket beside the *kapp* and apron she'd finished on Tuesday. The *kapp* would need starching and ironing, but the outfit would be ready for Naomi to wear at next Sunday's services. "I'm sorry if I upset everyone," she said. "But I have to decide for myself."

"Ya," Mam agreed. "You do. I know a little how you feel. When I chose your father, it was against my family's wishes. My father especially felt betrayed."

"Because you fell in love with Dat?"

Mam steepled her hands and tapped her chin gently with her fingertips. "Because, in marrying him, I chose the Old Order Amish faith over the one I was raised in."

"But you weren't turning your back on God."

"Ne, but my parents felt I was turning my back on the world."

"Have you ever been sorry?"

Her mother smiled, and Anna thought again how beautiful she was. "Not for a moment. It wasn't giving up life, so much as embracing it. Our way is a special blessing, and I thank God every day that this was the path He chose for me."

"You really believe that? That our Lord wanted you and Dat to marry?"

"With all my heart."

Anna sighed. "That's beautiful, Mam. It's what I want. To love someone like that. To have him love me. And to never wonder if I made the right decision."

"It's what you deserve." Mam rose and picked up Naomi's dress. "This is good work, Anna. And you've put in a deep hem. She'll start to shoot up soon. I think she will be slim like her mother, but tall like the women in her father's family. A sweet girl, Naomi. With a bright mind. She may make a teacher some day."

"I think she'd like that."

"It's good of you to take an interest in her. She's been a long time without a mother's care."

"So I told Samuel. Sometimes I think Naomi has had to grow up too quickly. She needs to be a child for a few years yet."

"It sounds to me as if you have a mother's interest in Samuel's girls."

"*Ya,* but I worry about the twins," Anna admitted. "It's clear that they don't want me to marry their father."

Mam folded Naomi's dress and laid it on the

bed. "They are children still, Anna. Sometimes you have to be tough."

"You never had any boys, Mam."

"Ne?" Her mother smiled. "I had brothers. And now we have Irwin. I think he has become my son, even if he was delivered a little late in life."

"Peter and Rudy don't want a new mother, and they don't want to share their father with a wife." She wouldn't tell Mam about the hurtful things the twins had said to her. That was her problem.

"Eleven-year-old boys can be difficult, but you'll work it out. I have faith in you."

More than I do, Anna thought.

"Do you want to go with me to the school board meeting? Samuel's coming to pick me up, so that I don't have to drive. We'll be planning the winter picnic, and we could use your ideas."

Anna shook her head. "It's not my place, Mam." She could guess what Mam was about. Her mother wanted to throw her and Samuel together. Anna hadn't seen him since their thrilling sleigh ride last Sunday, and the impulsive promise she'd made to allow him to court her seemed scary. She needed more time to think. "You go. I'll see to the house and pack your lunch for tomorrow."

Her mother turned toward the door. "Very well." Anna heard her sigh. "Sometimes you remind me so much of your father. It always took him forever to make up his mind about the least thing."

"And once he had?"

Mam chuckled. "And once he had, there was no wavering. Jonas would stand by his decision until fish grew in our garden and the hens laid cabbages."

Samuel had to pass the chair shop on his way to Hannah's farm, and he couldn't resist the opportunity to stop and chat with Roman before the others arrived. As satisfying as Sunday's sleigh ride had been, and as pleased as he was about Anna finally agreeing to the courtship, he was still worried. Her birthday was fast approaching, and he was growing impatient. What if she refused him? They were the talk of the community this week, and if she wouldn't have him, he'd be an object of jest for years to come.

He could protest that he didn't care what anyone thought, but he did. He valued the judgment of his friends and neighbors, and he wanted them to be supportive. He hoped he didn't look like a fool. He knew his sons weren't happy about his courting Anna, but he wasn't certain they would have welcomed any woman as their stepmother. He was afraid that he'd spoiled them.

Finding the fine line between being a responsible father and a doting one wasn't easy, and he'd found that each of his children was different. What worked with Lori Ann was exactly the wrong thing for Naomi or Mae. Even the twins had their own separate personalities. Peter tended to follow Rudy's lead; yet, left to his own devices, he could show more maturity than his brother. Samuel had always believed that when the children were older, it would be easier to be a father, but that wasn't so. He needed a partner more than ever, a woman to talk to and confide in. Anna was his first choice; but if he couldn't have her, he'd have to make the effort to find someone else…perhaps someone older and more settled.

He tied his horse to the hitching rail and went into the shop. Roman had brought in kerosene heaters and placed gas lamps on the oval table for the meeting. The shop had electricity, but there was no need for it tonight. Fannie had made heaps of *fastnachts,* a fried donut with nutmeg, and Roman had a kettle of sweet cider heating. In the shop, the board could talk as long and late as they pleased, without disrupting Fannie's routine of getting her children ready for bed.

Roman looked up from his ledger and smiled as Samuel entered the room. "Where's Hannah? I thought you were bringing her tonight?"

"I am, shortly. Just wanted to be sure you had those receipts I sent Peter over with last week."

"Right here." Roman waved to a chair. "Heard you made quite a sight on Sunday, in that fancy sleigh of yours. Wish I'd seen it."

"You heard about it, huh?" Samuel sat down. "So you know that Anna and I are walking out together."

Roman laughed. "You'd better be. And I'd best be hearing bans read in services soon. Martha was fit to be tied. Said it was scandalous, you two flying around the county with bells on."

"She would."

Roman offered him a mug of cider, but Samuel shook his head. "So you're set on Anna, are you?" Roman removed his glasses and looked hard at him. "You're sure this is right for both of you?"

"I am, but she's still nervous."

"About you, herself, or the children?"

Samuel leaned back and folded his arms. "She keeps talking about Frieda, about how pretty she was. Anna doesn't think I'll be satisfied with her, not after Frieda. I try to tell her different, but she's stubborn."

Roman sipped his own cider. "Comes by it honest. Her mother puts the *S* in stubborn when she sets her mind to it." He hesitated.

"Say what you're thinking," Samuel urged him.

"I hope you can work this out first. Otherwise you'll spend the rest of your life trying to make her believe that you see more in her than a strong back and a Plain face. Not loving oneself can tear up a marriage. I've seen it with my cousin and his wife. She inherited a farm, and he came there as a hired man. After they married, he worked it and made a go of it, but Zekey never felt like he was good enough."

"They still together?"

"Oh, sure. He's turned Beachy Amish, got a car, but they hold to their vows. Trouble is, neither one seems happy. It's sad when a man and wife don't fit together like a hand and glove. Hard on the children."

"But Anna Yoder. You think we can be happy together?" Samuel urged his friend.

"I think so. But it's not me, it's Anna you have to convince of that," Roman said. "Whatever you decide, I'll still be there for both of you."

It was after nine when the school board finished its business and made the final plans for the winter picnic. The event would begin in Samuel's barn, Saturday evening, in two weeks. The children would put on a program demonstrating to their parents what they had learned, and then there would be a spelling bee.

Next, Samuel would auction off baskets of cookies made by unmarried women and girls. The men and boys would bid on the baskets, and all the money would go toward the school. Each eligible young woman would pack supper to go with the cookies, and at the end of the evening, the couples would spread a blanket on the straw and share the food. Afterward, there would be games and singing. It would be well chaperoned, fun for everyone and a proven moneymaker for the school.

Hannah was excited with the prospect of the frolic. "Winter's bad weather keeps our young people in their homes too much. It's so important that they have a chance to mingle with others their own age," she said on the way home in Samuel's carriage.

"I agree," Samuel said, urging Smoky toward Hannah's house at the end of her lane.

"I'm glad the children have two weeks to study their spelling. Since you've offered to donate a calf to the top speller, competition will be fierce."

Samuel chuckled. "And maybe some of the parents who don't care too much about their kids' education will take a little more interest."

"You're a good man, Samuel," Hannah said, as he reined in his horse at her back door. "You give so much to the community. I hope everyone appreciates it."

"I have three children in the school and two more to follow. Why wouldn't I help as much as I can?" He got down and helped her out of the buggy. The ground was still muddy from the melted snow.

"Come in for coffee?" she asked.

He was about to decline when he saw Anna's face at the kitchen window. Their eyes met and his heart leaped in his chest. *"Ya,"* he said, hurrying to tie the horse to the rail. "Coffee would be good, after all that sweet cider.

"I'd like to drive Anna to church this Sunday," he said. "If it's all right with you." How was it that a man his age could feel like a boy again? Just the sight of Anna's sweet face made him giddy-headed.

Hannah called over her shoulder. "You'll have to ask her."

He followed her into the house, and there was a flurry of putting away of coats and scarves and mittens. Only Anna was in the kitchen, but it wouldn't have mattered if all her sisters, her grandmother and her aunts were there. Samuel had eyes only for Anna.

"What kind of cookies will you be baking for the winter picnic?" he asked her.

"What kind do you like best?"

"Sand tarts and black walnut cookies," he answered, "but I eat them all."

"Almond slices?"

"Love them."

Anna smiled. "I'll see what I can do."

"I suppose I'll have to pay a high price for your basket. Everyone knows how well you bake."

Anna dimpled and blushed. "You can't bid on mine. You'll be the auctioneer."

"Don't care. Nobody gets your basket but me."

Somehow, in the exchange, Hannah had left the kitchen. He hadn't even seen her go.

"Would you like coffee?" she asked.

He nodded. He would have drank vinegar, if it meant he got to sit here at the table, in this warm, cozy spot, with her. He took his seat at the head of the table while she brought him a steaming cup and a slice of lemon meringue pie. "Mmm," he said. "Looks delicious. If you keep on like this, I won't be able to fit through the barn door."

"Ne," she said softly. "You work too hard, Samuel. You'll not get fat."

The sound of his name on her lips made him want to pull her into his arms and hug her, but he didn't dare. Instead, he took a bite of the pie. It was as good as it looked.

"I wanted to ask you a favor," Anna said, coming to sit at the table with him. "I want you to speak to Bishop Atlee for me. It's about Grossmama."

He listened as she explained Lovina's desire to go to the English senior center. He didn't speak until she'd finished.

"I don't see what harm it would do," Anna said. "It would make her feel useful."

Samuel hated to deny Anna anything, but what was she thinking? They didn't send their old people to be cared for by the English. They kept them at home, no matter how ill or feeble they became.

"So what do you think?" she asked. "Will you speak to the bishop for me?"

"I know that you care for your grandmother more than even some of her own daughters seem to do. But this is not our way, Anna. You know that. It would be useless to take such a question to Bishop Atlee. He wouldn't permit it."

Anna stood up. "So you won't ask him for me?" Her voice was no longer sweet, but firm.

He loved her, but he couldn't allow her to force him to do something he knew wasn't right. It wouldn't do to start their marriage off by letting her think that he could be led around by the nose like a prize bull. "There would be no need," he said firmly and he left it at that.

Chapter Fifteen

On Sunday, Samuel and the children came to drive Anna to services. Anna held Mae on her lap and Lori Ann sat on the seat between them. Irwin had taken Naomi's dress and *kapp* over on Saturday, so the girl was able to wear her new outfit to church. Anna was pleased to see that it fit her so well. Being with Samuel and his family seemed right, and despite the glares she received from the twins, Anna felt comfortable as they reached the Beachy farm and were caught up in the familiar day of worship and fellowship.

As always, the hymns and preaching soothed Anna and made her feel that all was right with the world. Mae seemed content to be held, and when she and Lori Ann grew restless, Susanna was there to take the two children to the kitchen for milk and a snack. When they returned, Miriam produced a handkerchief doll from her pocket for each girl to play with, and soon Mae drifted off to sleep in Anna's arms.

Maybe, if I married Samuel, it wouldn't be so different, Anna thought. *I wouldn't be leaving my family, just stretching my arms to include more people that I love.* She knew that she loved Samuel's children, but did she love Samuel the way a woman ought to love a man? Did he love her that way? She knew there were different kinds of love. Were there different kinds of love between married couples, too?

Miriam's tug on her sleeve broke Anna from her reverie, and she realized that everyone was rising for one of the closing hymns. Mae stirred and made a soft little sigh, then nestled against her. Anna smiled down at the child as a warm surge of emotion enveloped her. *She could be mine,* Anna thought. *They could all be mine...even Samuel.*

She closed her eyes and prayed fervently for guidance.

There had been no time alone, after services and the communal Sunday meal, for Anna to try to convince Samuel to reconsider talking to the bishop for her. Samuel drove her home and then hurried to his own farm to begin the evening chores. Anna really wanted to speak with Samuel on the matter, because she didn't feel he'd given her plan fair consideration. Who could possibly believe that Grossmama wasn't being taken care of properly? Anyone who knew her should be able to see that hers was a special case, and that teaching Englishers how to make her rugs would only restore her sense of being useful.

Monday was wash day, and too busy for Anna to find time to do something about her idea, but late on Tuesday afternoon, when Grossmama was taking her nap, Anna walked across the fields to Samuel's house with a mind to plead her case to him again. She didn't see anyone in the farmyard, and she doubted that Samuel would be in the house at that time of day. Hesitantly, she pushed open the heavy barn door and called his name. "Samuel? It's Anna. Are you here?"

She heard a rustle and what sounded like a giggle, but there was no sign of Samuel. She entered the barn and pulled the door closed behind her. Light poured through a glass window at one end of the hayloft, but otherwise, it was shadowy and dark inside. Horses stood in their stalls, and the boys' pony nickered. "Samuel?"

Something flew past Anna's head. Splat! Puzzled, she turned to see a smashed egg oozing down the side of the pony's box stall. As her eyes adjusted, she caught a glimpse of a white face and blond hair before another egg came sailing down from above, out of the hayloft, and just missed her shoulder. "Rudy?" she shouted. "Is that you? You're supposed to be in school!"

"Not Rudy," Peter called from the feed room. "It's me!" He drew back his arm and hurled a dead mouse, of all things, at her. He leaped out into the passageway, stuck out his tongue and taunted, "Fatty-fatty, two by four!" Then he darted into the dark shadows again.

Anna almost laughed out loud. It was time she and the boys had a little talk, and this would be the perfect opportunity. If Peter was on the ground floor, Rudy could only be one place. The direction the second egg had come from: up. Stripping off her coat and bonnet, she dropped them onto the nearest hay bale. She might be a big girl, but she was strong, and she could move fast when she wanted to. Rudy wasn't going to escape. There was only one way out of the loft—down the ladder.

Anna strode across the barn and took the ladder, one rung at a time. Behind her, Peter was shouting, "Can't catch me, can't catch me," but she had no intentions of trying. Rudy was the main mischief maker, and if she caught him, she wouldn't have to go after his twin.

When she reached the top of the ladder, she saw Rudy climbing a stack of hay bales. Pigeons flew up and feathers and dust sprayed the boy as he climbed higher, toward the roof. He'd lost his hat, and when one pigeon dropped a smear of excrement on his head, Anna burst into laughter. Scrambling, Rudy reached the top of the hay pile, and the whole structure began to sway.

"Best you get down here and take your medicine before you fall and break your neck," Anna warned. "You know your father is going to find out you skipped school." She waited, arms folded, beside the hatch that opened to the ladder.

"Not coming down," Rudy said. He wiped at the gooey mess in his hair and grimaced. "You can't make me."

"I don't have to," Anna said. "All I have to do is wait here until your dat comes in for evening milking. Then you can explain why you're wasting good eggs, knocking down his hay bales and being rude to a guest."

"We don't like you." Peter came slowly up the ladder behind her and poked his head into the loft.

"You don't have to like me." Anna looked from one twin to the other. "You have to respect me."

"We don't want Dat to marry you," Rudy said. "Naomi says Dat is going to marry you and then you'll be our mother." His voice was tight, as if he was about to burst into tears.

"Ah," Anna said. "You two think you know better than your father, when it comes to deciding what he should do?"

"You aren't our mother." Peter walked around Anna to stand closer to his brother. "She was pretty."

"Ya," Anna agreed. "Your mother was beautiful, and a good woman, a good mother. But she's in heaven now, and your father needs help with the house and with the little girls. You two are almost grown. You may not need a mother, but you might need a friend."

Rudy slid halfway down the pile. "We don't need anybody."

Anna sighed. "You must trust your father." When neither boy answered, she went on. "Tell me something. If he came to the bottom of the ladder right this minute and said 'jump'—if he held up his arms to catch you, would you trust him?"

Peter frowned.

"You would jump, wouldn't you?" she pressed. "Because you trust him to do the right thing. So you have to trust him now. If he chooses me or another woman to be his new wife, you must try to understand. He's the adult and your father, and you still live under his roof. You have to trust his decisions."

"You gonna tell on us?" Rudy asked. "Not about school. We'll tell him that. About the eggs?"

"Should I?" Anna replied.

"We'll be in big trouble," Peter said. "More than last time." Rudy slid the rest of the way down the hay. Peter looked at him and wrinkled his nose. "You stink," he said.

"Pigeon poo."

"Maybe that's fair punishment for throwing eggs at me." Anna's gaze narrowed. "Think about what I said. Think about your father and sisters, and about what's best for your family. You're growing older, both of you. Maybe you should find a way to do good instead of causing trouble. Maybe that would make your mother happy."

Rudy was red-faced, sniffing and wiping at his dirty face with the back of his hands. "Sorry," he said.

She turned her gaze on Peter. "And by the way, Peter. You're right," she said. "I am fat, but it still hurts my feelings when you call me names. It makes me cry at night. Did you like it when the other boys teased you at school for failing your spelling test?"

Peter shook his head. *"Ne."*

"At your age, you should be thinking about what kind of men you want to be when you are grown. Do you want to be someone like your dat? Because if you do, it's time to start changing your ways."

Anna stood there for a minute looking at both of them, then climbed down the ladder and put on her coat and bonnet. "I'd clean up those eggs if I were you," she hollered up to the twins. "And if you try something like that with me again, I promise you'll not get off as easily."

She was halfway back across the field toward home when she realized that she hadn't found Samuel and wasn't any closer to helping Grossmama than before. She didn't know if she'd made things worse between her and the boys or better, but she was through taking their nonsense. From now on, she would be the adult. But mature as she was, she couldn't help but take satisfaction from the memory of Rudy wiping pigeon poo out of his hair.

Twice that week Samuel and the children came to dinner at the Yoder home, and he was heartened by the way his girls ran to Anna to be hugged and fussed over. Hannah and her family treated him as though he was already family, and the twins were on their best behavior. But as much as he wished it, there was no opportunity for him to spend time alone with Anna.

He needed very much to talk to her. She was as warm and friendly as ever to him, and he couldn't have asked for anyone to be kinder to his daughters. But there was a distance between them that hadn't been there the day he'd taken her riding in the sleigh. She was obviously upset about the matter of Lovina and the English senior center, but surely Anna wouldn't allow that to come between them, would she?

He'd written to his sisters in Ohio, and told them that he was courting Anna Yoder, and that they should be expecting an invitation to a wedding soon. Normally, weddings were held in late autumn, but since he was a widower, he could marry when it was most convenient, so long as the proper bans were called and the church leaders were in agreement. Anna was young, but she was of age, and she'd never been married before. There was no reason they couldn't become a married couple before spring planting.

Sunday was a visiting day, and Samuel hoped to be able to leave the children in Hannah's care and take Anna in the buggy to visit friends in the neighborhood. Maybe then he could talk about their little disagreement and get past it. With each day, Samuel was more and more convinced that Anna was exactly the right wife for him, and that he could make her happy.

Earlier in the week, he'd ordered ice cream from a delivery truck and had it stored in the freezer at the chair shop. After dinner, he'd drive down and pick it up, so that they could all enjoy a special treat. His hogs had come back from the butcher in neat packages, and the meal the two families had shared had centered around fresh pork chops that he had brought to Hannah's the day before. Soon, he hoped to be able to have Anna's mother, sisters and extended family to his home for dinners. Other than his children, he had no relatives here in Delaware, and with Anna's help, he couldn't wait to play host.

But once again Samuel was disappointed. Anna agreed to come with him, but just when they were about to depart, Bishop Atlee, his wife and sister arrived to pay a call on the Yoders. In a buggy behind them came Martha, Dorcas and Reuben. There was no question of Samuel's leaving, and the whole group ended up spending the afternoon in Hannah's parlor. It was a pleasant time, as the bishop was known for his sense of humor, and always had a store of new jokes and news from far-off communities. But it wasn't the way Samuel would have chosen to spend the hours.

Finally, when everyone had stuffed themselves on cake and ice cream and consumed pots of strong coffee, Bishop Atlee rose and began to make his goodbyes. "Oh, Samuel," he said as he reached for his coat. "You'll be pleased to know that I've come to a decision on Anna's request." His eyes were twinkling.

Confused, Samuel glanced at Anna and saw that she'd blushed a rosy red. He returned his attention to what the bishop was saying.

"Quite an unusual request, this. I can tell you that I prayed over it several nights." His expression grew serious. "You did know about Anna's coming to see me on Friday, didn't you?"

Samuel shook his head.

"But she *has* spoken to you about Lovina's request to take part in the program at the Englisher senior center?"

"*Ya,*" Samuel answered, as it dawned on him that what he was talking about was that Anna had gone to the bishop herself, after Samuel had refused her. He bristled. "I told her that it wasn't our way, that we kept our old people at home."

"And who are you to say where I should go or not go?" Lovina demanded.

"Mother!" Martha admonished. "You don't talk so to the bishop."

"He's young enough to be my son, and I'll say whatever I please. I want to go and teach the Englishers how to make proper rugs."

"There, there." Bishop Atlee broke into a wide smile and raised his hand. "And so you shall, Lovina. I doubt we have to worry about you straying from the fold, do we? You might even teach the worldly folk a thing or two in the process."

He glanced back at Samuel, who didn't know what to say.

"Come, don't be such a stick-in-the-mud." The bishop grasped Samuel's arm. "We may be a conservative church, but we aren't backward. We don't turn our back on the Englisher doctors or hospitals, do we? And as Anna has so ably pointed out to me, Lovina isn't going two days a week to be cared for, but to teach and relieve the spirits of others. I think it's a fine plan, and if she wants to ride in the red van, she has my blessing."

All the way home, Samuel kept thinking about what Anna had done. Where had she gotten the spunk to go to Bishop Atlee on her own, and how had she convinced him to break with tradition and allow such a thing? A part of Samuel was annoyed; he'd been embarrassed to hear the news from the bishop first. But a part of him couldn't help but be pleased with Anna. Most women would have trusted his word as a deacon, but she'd gone to a higher authority. As was her right as a member of the church, and maybe her duty to do all she could for her grandmother.

Still, he felt a little foolish.

Was this how it would be, once they were married? Would she challenge his authority in the household? Frieda never would have. What was he getting himself into?

Unconsciously, Johanna's husband's words came back into his mind. *"Hannah's too liberal. She's spoiled her girls. They don't know their place."*

A man had to be the head of the house. It was the way he'd been raised and what he believed. A wife should heed her husband's advice. And he'd

made it quite clear to Anna that he didn't think
that sending her grandmother to the English was
a good idea. Yet, she'd gone and asked the bishop
herself. It stuck in his craw like a fish bone.

Anna had always seemed so sweet and easygoing. Had he misjudged her? Yet, Anna hadn't
challenged him or argued. She'd simply persisted,
and apparently made a good case to the bishop,
good enough to get his approval. Samuel wished
Reuben and Martha hadn't heard it all. It would be
common knowledge in the community by tomorrow. It would be a long time before his neighbors
quit calling him "stick-in-the-mud".

By the time Samuel had finished the evening
milking, sent the hired man on his way and tucked
Mae and Lori Ann into bed, the worst of his an-
noyance had passed. Anna was, after all, very
young. He loved her, and this was something they
could work out. She just had to understand that she
had put him in a bad position, going over his head
and not telling him. It was natural that a couple
have some disagreements, and this would be easily
mended.

She must have known that he was unhappy. He'd
seen the distress in her eyes when he'd said his
goodbyes and left her mother's house. Doubtless,
Anna was already regretting her hasty decision to
go to the bishop after Samuel had been clear in his
opinion on the whole matter.

Samuel knew he didn't have it in him to be harsh with Anna, but it would be best if he nipped this misguided independence early on. He'd stay away from the Yoder house for a few days. When he didn't come she'd know why, and she'd quickly seek him out to make things right between them.

As much as he enjoyed being with Anna, and as much as it would hurt him not to be with her, he'd have to be firm. She had to remember that he was a church deacon, that he had to set an example for other members of the community. And Anna, as his wife, would have to do likewise. It wouldn't do to have the deacon's wife running about the county, going against her husband's wishes and making him look bad.

By Saturday's school program and cookie auction next weekend, they'd both be laughing about this incident. Anna would have learned from her mistake, and nothing like this would ever happen again.

Chapter Sixteen

Samuel didn't come to visit on Monday or Tuesday, and he didn't come on Wednesday or Thursday, although his hired man stopped by in the afternoon to bring ten pounds of bacon, a fresh loin of pork, fifty pounds of potatoes and two blocks of scrapple. Leah stowed the gifts in the refrigerator as Anna continued rolling out dough for Saturday's cookie bake. "Wonder why Samuel didn't bring them himself?" Leah asked, with a twinkle in her eye.

Anna chuckled. "You know why. You saw him on Sunday afternoon, when Bishop Atlee called him a stick-in-the-mud. Samuel Mast's nose is out of joint because I persuaded the bishop to let Grossmama go to the English center."

Leah grinned. "You've hurt his manly feelings, Anna."

"All I did was check with the bishop myself,"

Anna replied, choosing a cookie cutter in the shape of a cow, and beginning to cut out cookies and slide them onto a baking sheet.

"You think he's angry with you for doing that?"

Anna shrugged. "I think his pride is a little bruised that I didn't take his word on the matter."

Leah brought a second cookie sheet to the table. "What if he's still upset by Saturday—what if he doesn't bid on your basket?"

"Then I'll give the cookies to the children. It was right that Grossmama got to go. She might not like the senior center once she's there, but that's up to her." Anna slapped another lump of dough on the floured board and began to roll it out with a wooden rolling pin that her father had made for her mother when they were first married. "If Samuel wants to marry me, he should know who I am. I don't have Miriam's temper or your courage out in the world, but I won't be quiet when I think I'm right. Even if I wasn't right and the bishop had said no, at least then I would know I had tried my best. I don't think Samuel would have been so annoyed if the bishop had said no."

"I think you're right," Aunt Jezebel said as she came into the kitchen. "You know, that's what I always admired most about your mother. She was a good wife to your father, but she never let him get too big for his britches." Her face flushed a delicate pink. "I didn't mean to listen in, but Lovina fell asleep, and I thought I'd come to give you a hand with the cookie baking."

Anna smiled at the little woman. "We can use your help," she said. "You always made the best black walnut cookies, and Irwin cracked and hulled two cupfuls of nuts from the big tree at the end of the garden last night."

Aunt Jezebel hesitated before coming to hug Anna. "It was a brave thing you did, speaking to your bishop. A kind thing for Lovina. It will make her feel useful. Better for her to be out among people, sewing her rugs, than always sitting in your kitchen finding fault. I think she will be happier."

"So you don't think I was wrong to go to the bishop?" Anna asked.

Her aunt dusted a bit of flour off Anna's chin. "*Ne,* love, I don't. And I think your young man will see that, once he's had time to cool down."

"I wouldn't want him to think I was forward," Anna said. "To go against his wishes… A man should be the head of the house."

"And the woman the heart." Aunt Jezebel looked into Anna's eyes. "He's a fool if he lets you slip away. You will make Samuel Mast and his motherless children happy."

"You really think so?" Anna asked.

Her aunt pursed her lips. "What do you see

when you look at your Grossmama? Do you see her wrinkles or her thinning hair?"

Anna shook her head. "I see her like she was when I was a child. She always walked so straight, and her bonnet and apron were so stiff they crinkled when she walked. I thought she was wonderfully Plain."

Aunt Jezebel smiled. "You really love my sister, don't you?"

"Ya," Anna said. "I do. She can be grouchy, but inside I know she wants to be kind."

"You see Lovina that way because you have love in your heart for her. Many a fair face hides a sour disposition. You are beautiful inside, Anna. And if your Samuel can't see that, he doesn't deserve you."

"I agree," Leah slid a pan of cookies into the oven. "You always think of other people before you think of yourself. Besides, if you don't say yes, Samuel might be desperate enough to end up with Dorcas. And she wouldn't be able to manage those five kids—not to mention her biscuits." Leah giggled. "The last batch she made were so awful, Aunt Martha said the chickens wouldn't even eat them."

Saturday evening finally arrived, and containers of food and baskets of cookies had been stowed in the back of the big Yoder buggy. Irwin, Leah and Rebecca had walked over to Samuel's to help make last minute preparations for the get-together. Miriam and Charley invited Susanna to ride with them, leaving Mam, Anna, Aunt Jezebel and Grossmama to take the family buggy.

Anna had been looking forward to parents' night and the cookie auction as much as anyone, but not hearing from Samuel all week had made her nervous. She wanted him to outbid everyone for her basket, and she wanted to see his children recite their pieces, take part in the spelling bee and show what they had learned this term in class. Most of all, she wanted to sit on a blanket in the barn with Samuel and the other unmarried couples, and share laughter, as well as the contents of her picnic.

She'd been so worried that she wondered if she should walk over to Samuel's house and tell him that she was sorry. Mam had put an end to that idea.

"Are you sorry that your Grossmama is going next week in the red van?" Mam had asked. "If you had it to do over again, would you still take your case to Bishop Atlee?"

Anna had nodded slowly. "I suppose I would."

"Exactly," Mam said. "So if there's any apologizing to be done, it should be Samuel Mast who does it, not you."

Anna hadn't gone to Samuel, but neither had she slept much last night. What if he was still angry with her? What if he ignored her and bid on some other girl's basket? What if he wouldn't speak to her? Before, when she was resigned to being unmarried, she'd come to accept it. But Samuel's courting had opened up a whole armful of wanting. If she lost him forever, she didn't think she could bear it.

She looked at the clock for the third time in the last thirty minutes. "We'd best be going, hadn't we?" she asked.

Mam smiled at her. "It's early yet, but it won't hurt. Find Grossmama's black bonnet and help her into her heavy cape."

"I'm sick," Grossmama whimpered when Anna went to her room to find her. The old woman lay on her bed, her face pale, eyes fluttering weakly. "I'm having a dizzy spell. I tripped and…"

"Oh, Grossmama, did you hurt yourself? Why didn't you call us?" Anna ran to her and laid a palm on her forehead. Her grandmother's skin felt cool to the touch, but a fall could have injured her bad hip again. "Mam!" she shouted. "Come here." Anna poured water from the bedside pitcher into a glass. "Would you like a drink?"

"*Ne.* My head hurts. Let me lie here and try to sleep."

"I hate to have you miss the evening. Aunt Martha and Aunt Alma will be there."

"I couldn't go out on such a cold night. It will

be the death of me. You all go to your frolic. Don't worry about me."

After her mother and Aunt Jezebel had joined Anna at Lovina's bedside, the three withdrew to the kitchen. "What do you think?" Mam asked Jezebel. "Is she really ill?" She glanced at the clock. "As much as I'd like to, I can't stay with her. The children and their families will be arriving soon at the gathering. As their teacher, I need to be there."

"Anna!" Grossmama called in a surprisingly strong voice. "Bring me a cup of chamomile tea."

Aunt Jezebel sighed. "I'll stay. I don't know whether this is real or not. She always says she's dizzy or sick when she doesn't want to go somewhere or do something. You and Anna go on." Anna could see the disappointment on her aunt's face. She loved getting out of the house and visiting with other women in the community, and she loved watching the children recite.

"Anna!" Grossmama called. "I need you."

The sound of a glass shattering brought Aunt Jezebel to her feet. "Let me go in to her," she insisted. "I can usually calm her when she has one of her spells."

But Grossmama would have none of it, and fifteen minutes later, when the buggy rolled out of the yard, it was Mam and Aunt Jezebel who were going to the parents' night program, and Anna who was sweeping up the last of the broken glass.

She'd forced a smile and insisted that she didn't mind, but inside she wanted to weep. She'd wanted so badly to be with Samuel tonight, and now she wouldn't have the chance to make everything right with him. And even if they patched up their disagreement later, tonight would be gone forever.

"Anna!" Grossmama called shrilly as Anna carried the broken glass to the kitchen trashcan. "Where's my tea?"

Anna sighed and turned to the cupboard. She took down the can of chamomile tea and carried it to the counter. Maybe it was best that she didn't go tonight, she thought. That way, if Samuel was still angry with her, she wouldn't be embarrassed in front of everyone. Besides, if she'd left her grandmother and the woman really had been ill, she'd never forgive herself.

An hour later, Grossmama's dizziness seemed to have passed, and she felt well enough to have a bowl of chicken soup, some applesauce and three oatmeal cookies leftover from the bounty that had been baked for the school program. "You're a good girl," her grandmother said, patting Anna's hand. "You're the only one who cares about me."

"That's not true," Anna replied. "Lots of people love you. Mam and Aunt Jezebel, my sisters, and…"

"Not like you," Grossmama insisted. "You're the

only one who listened to me when I said I wanted to go to the Englisher center. Everyone else thinks I'm a crazy old lady…just because I get confused… forget things. You will, too, when you're my age."

Anna patted her hand. "I don't think you're crazy, and neither does Mam."

"And…" Tears welled in the elderly woman's faded blue eyes. "Because sometimes I make believe my Jonas is alive…when I know he's not."

Anna fought tears, her heart touched by her grandmother's revelation. "I can't imagine how hard it must be to have lost so many people you love. But…" She took a deep breath and said what she'd wanted to say since Grossmama had first come to stay with them. "You should try to be kinder to those who love you—to Mam, especially. She does her best to care for you and…and you…" She couldn't say more. Reverence for the elderly was too ingrained in her. It wasn't her place to lecture her grandmother, but it was so difficult to see her and Mam always at odds.

There was a long pause, and then her grandmother nodded. "*Ya, ya,* I know. Hannah is more of a daughter to me than my own blood daughters, but it isn't easy to live in a daughter-in-law's house."

"It's Dat's house, too. Your son's house."

Grossmama's mouth tightened. "And how much

do I see him? He's always in the barn. Those cows must be milked dry."

Anna blinked. A moment ago her grandmother had said that she knew Dat was dead, but now… Was she pretending now, or had the fog closed in on her mind again? "Mam wants you here," she said. "We all do."

"I suppose I can try harder." Grossmama yawned. "For Jonas's sake, not Hannah's."

Anna leaned close and pulled the quilt up around the old woman's shoulders. "Sleep for a little while. I'm sure it will make you feel better."

"Don't leave me. I don't want to be alone in this big house."

"I won't leave the house. I'll be right in the kitchen."

"If Jonas comes in, tell him I want to talk to him." Her grandmother closed her eyes. Soon her breathing grew heavy. The lines in her face relaxed and she began to snore. Anna rose and quietly left the room.

In the kitchen, she washed the cup and dishes that Grossmama had eaten from and lit a gas lamp. Carefully, she carried it into the parlor and set it on the wide windowsill, taking care to tuck the curtain away from the glass chimney. "To bring you all safely home," she whispered.

The children's program would be over by now, and the bidding on the cookie baskets would be next. She wondered how Naomi had done in the spelling bee. Her spelling was quite good, but Anna wasn't sure if it was good enough to win against children who were several grades ahead of her. She'd wanted to be there for Naomi and for the twins as well. Anna hoped the talk she'd had with them in Samuel's hayloft would help. She didn't worry about the two younger girls. Susanna and Rebecca would watch over them and see they didn't miss out on anything, but Naomi could sometimes be shy around the other children in the community. It was easy for her to be overlooked. Anna should have reminded Aunt Jezebel to be sure that Naomi didn't feel neglected.

Anna glanced in on her grandmother, who seemed to be sleeping peacefully. Maybe the hectic evening and the cold night air *would* have been too much for her.

She returned to the kitchen and looked around to see if anything needed doing. The others wouldn't be home for more than an hour. It was too early for her to go to bed, and she wasn't in the mood for sewing. She took Dat's old barn coat off the hook and stepped out onto the back porch. Everything was still beneath the full, silver moon; not a sound came from the barn or the chicken house.

"Oh, Samuel," she murmured into the darkness. "I wanted to be with you tonight." Salt tears stung the backs of her eyelids and she blinked them away.

And then, just as she'd turned to go back into the house, she heard the faint sound of a horse's hooves on the frozen dirt lane. *Clippity-clop. Clippity-clop.*

Anna's pulse quickened. It was too soon for Mam, Aunt Jezebel and the girls to be coming back. Unless something had gone wrong... Was someone else ill, or had there been an accident? She hurried across the porch and down the back steps into the yard. Had she imagined the sound? No, she could definitely make out the creak of buggy wheels and the hard rhythm of a pacer coming fast.

But the horse and buggy that appeared around the corner of the house wasn't Mam's. It was Samuel's.

He reined the horse in only an arm's length from where she stood. "Anna? What are you doing out here in the cold? I nearly ran you down."

She laughed. *Samuel! Samuel was here!* He'd come to find her. "Not likely," she managed.

He climbed down out of the buggy and came toward her. He was so tall, so broad and sturdy in the moonlight. "I waited, but you didn't come," he said.

"I wanted to come," she said. Her hands were

trembling so hard that she tucked them behind her back. "But Grossmama took sick and..."

"Your sisters told me." He looked down, then up again. "I was wrong, Anna, to be upset that you went to the bishop. All week I thought about it. I was wrong. You were right to talk to Bishop Atlee for your grandmother."

"I didn't mean to make you angry. I just wanted to be sure I had done all I could for Grossmama."

"As you should have. Anna, Anna. Just when I think I have you figured out, you surprise me. You're wonderful, did you know that? Wonderful."

Pleased but flustered, she took a step back, searching for a safer subject. "Naomi," she seized upon. "How did she do in the spelling bee?"

"First place," he said with a chuckle. "My own daughter won the heifer."

Anna laughed with him. "She's smart, Samuel, like her father." She swallowed the constriction in her throat. "But why are you here? The evening can't be over. Everyone must still be at your place."

"And so they are." He turned back to the buggy, returned a minute later with a blanket and two baskets. "I put your cookies up first, bid fifty dollars on them, and no one else made an offer."

"Fifty dollars?" The tears were back, but this time they were tears of happiness. "You paid fifty dollars for my cookies?"

"I would have paid more, if anyone had bid against me. And if you couldn't come to the picnic, I'm bringing the picnic to you. Come now, before we freeze out here. Take these baskets. I'll put my horse in the shed and follow you in."

She nodded, too full of excitement to speak. *Samuel had come!* He wanted to be with her. He'd left the frolic for her, and he'd bought her cookies for more money than anyone had ever paid. It might be *Hochmut,* pride, but it filled her with joy that he'd done such a thing. It couldn't be the cookies. It had to be *her* that he valued, Plain Anna Yoder. *Samuel valued her!*

They spread Samuel's blanket on the kitchen floor, opened the door to the wood stove, and built up the fire. Then, by the light of a single lamp, they laughed and talked and ate the food that she'd packed. Samuel told her about his plans for spring planting and his desire to buy horses for Peter and Rudy. "They're getting too long-legged for the pony," he explained.

"And what will you do with the pony?" Anna asked. Despite all the goodies spread around them, she'd been too excited to eat. He must have felt the same way, because, for once, he wasn't eating much either. They were too busy talking.

"I was thinking that Naomi might like it. Not to ride astride, not for a girl."

"Ya," Anna agreed. "But she could use the pony

cart. It would be good for her to learn to drive. She spends too much time in the house with her books."

"I wanted to ask Lovina if she would teach Naomi to make braided rugs."

His words made her smile. "You like my grandmother, don't you? In spite of her sharp tongue?"

Samuel chuckled. "She reminds me of my Grossmama. You couldn't get away with anything around that one, I can tell you. *Ya.* I do like Lovina. And so do my girls. Despite her words sometimes, she always shows them kindness."

"I'm glad to hear you say that, because I've been thinking."

"About my proposal of marriage?" His voice grew husky. "Your birthday will be soon, Anna. You promised me an answer. Will you marry me?" He took hold of her hand and held it in his big one. "Beautiful Anna Yoder, will you do me the honor of becoming my wife?"

She opened her mouth to protest, to tell him that she wasn't beautiful, that he didn't have to say so when it wasn't true, and then all the things that Mam and Grossmama and Aunt Jezebel and her sisters had reminded her about inner beauty came rushing back. And suddenly it didn't matter that she was Plain anymore. Suddenly, she was so full of happiness that she could hardly speak.

"How much do you want to marry me?" she

asked. "Enough to take my grandmother as part of the package? I want to be with you, Samuel. I want to take care of you and the children, and I want to be a good and true wife to you, so long as I live." She paused to catch her breath. "But could you... would you consider having my Grossmama come to live with us? I think she would be happier there, with the little ones. I know it's a lot to ask, but—"

"You'll have me?" He grabbed her and pulled her against him in a great bear hug, then slowly lowered his head and kissed her tenderly on the lips. "I love you, my Anna," he said. "And if you'll take me, a man with five children, you can bring a dozen grandmothers to our home if you wish. You can bring your Aunt Jezebel, your sister Susanna, even your cousin Dorcas if you want."

Mouth tingling from the kiss, Anna touched his warm cheek and found it damp with tears. "Are you crying, Samuel?"

"I am," he admitted. "But don't tell anyone."

"I won't bring Dorcas, I promise."

He chuckled, stood and caught both her hands, lifting her up. "So you will marry me?"

"I said I would, didn't I?"

"When?" he asked.

"As soon as the bans can be properly read. You are a deacon in the church. We must set a good example for the young people."

"We could be married by spring."

"Whatever you say, Samuel," she replied sweetly. Every doubt had vanished. And in her heart, she was certain that this was the path that God had planned for her all along.

Epilogue

Anna rose from the big bed she shared with Samuel, and padded barefoot, in her long, white cotton nightgown, across the thick, braided rug. In the east, the first rays of dawn would soon appear and the roosters would be crowing to welcome the new day. In the darkness, she found her nightstand, removed her nightcap and brushed out her hair. Any minute, Samuel would be up to begin the morning chores, the children would tumble sleepily out of their beds and Grossmama would wake and want her morning cup of chamomile tea.

Anna smiled. She loved this time, when all the house was silent and the day full of possibilities waited like an unopened birthday gift. This was her home, her wonderful husband, her children and her grandmother. She never expected to be this happy in her marriage. She'd hoped she might be, but the reality of life with Samuel was better than she could have dreamed.

Deftly, she rolled her long hair into a bun and pinned it at the back of her head, before reaching for her freshly starched *kapp* and covering her head with it. The sweet, rich smells of spring wafted through the open window: plowed earth, apple blossoms, freshly cut grass and the first blooms of climbing roses.

Anna knelt and bowed her head in a moment of silent prayer, as she did every morning. God had answered all of her prayers, and her heart was full of praise for His many blessings. She knew that she and Samuel would face trials; every family did. But with each other, with faith and hard work, she was confident that they would overcome each obstacle.

As she rose to draw back the simple white curtain, Samuel called from the bed. "Anna, where are you?"

"Here, sleepyhead. Making ready for the day, as *you* should. The cows will be wanting milking and the sheep must be fed before breakfast."

"Come back to me, my sweet *kuchen*."

She heard him pat the bed beside him and she smiled. This was the teasing game they played every morning, and neither of them ever tired of it. "What, with so much to do, lazybones? It will be midmorning before I get the coffee on."

"Just for a minute, Anna."

Laughing, she returned to the high-poster bed

that had been Samuel's great grandfather's and slid in beside him. Samuel put his arm around her and drew her close, and she tucked her head against his shoulder.

"Mmm," he murmured. "This is nice. Can't we just stay here all day?"

"*Ne,* we cannot." She giggled. "What would the community say if their deacon lounged in his bed while the spring day was wasted?"

"I suppose you're right." He yawned. "I've been thinking, my Anna."

"*Ya,* Samuel. I'm sure you have."

"I think there's too much for you to do in this house. Your grandmother, the children, your garden. I have the boys and the hired man, but Naomi and Lori Ann are too young to be of much help."

"Hush." She placed two fingers over his lips. "To say such a thing about your daughters. They are good girls who show great promise of being better housewives than I am."

"No one could be a better wife or mother than you."

"Hush, Samuel. You will make me blush with such talk."

"All well, but I have decided. You must have help. My niece has more girls than her house can hold. If you agree, we'll ask her to send one or two to help you out."

Anna found his hand and squeezed it. "You are

too good to me. But there's no need. If you think I need help, let's ask my sister Rebecca to come for a few hours every day. She knows the way I like things in my kitchen, and she'll be good with the children."

"You've asked her already, I suppose," he said with a chuckle.

"Of course, Samuel. But if it doesn't please you, I can—"

"It pleases me very much, Anna. And if you'd rather have your sister than one of my nieces, that's exactly what we'll do. But you will have help. I'll not have you working your hands to the bone for us."

Anna laughed. "Small chance of that. What other husband in Kent County regularly scrubs his wife's kitchen floor?" She wiggled free of his embrace and slid across the bed. "Now, get up before the twins, or they'll never let you hear the end of it." She found her night robe on the chair and put it on.

"Do I have to?" he groaned.

She rested her fists on her ample hips. "*Ya,* Samuel. You have to. As you do every day."

He sat up and halfheartedly tossed a pillow in her direction. "Have I told you that I love you, woman?"

"Every day," she answered.

"You bring joy to this house."

"And you, Samuel, bring joy to my heart."

And, as was their custom, he rose and dressed, and they went down the wide staircase together, hand in hand, like young newlyweds, which was, she supposed, exactly what they were.

* * * * *

Dear Reader,

Welcome again to Seven Poplars, Delaware, home of the Old Order Amish family, the Yoders, and their friends and family. Anna's story is particularly dear to me because, unlike her sisters, she isn't beautiful by contemporary standards, not even in the Amish community. But beauty, we know, is in the eye of the beholder. Widower Samuel Mast has always seen Anna for her beauty within, and is eager to make her his wife. Anna has secretly adored Samuel and his children for years. The question is, can Anna, can any of us, truly love another if we do not love ourselves?

I hope you'll enjoy reading Anna's story as much as I've enjoyed writing it. As I came to know and love Anna Yoder, I was amazed by the wisdom and quiet and abiding faith in God that she displayed. I think you'll agree that plump Anna, the plain sister, is a special young woman.

Please come back and join me for Leah Yoder's story. After a year in Ohio, caring for her aging grandmother, she's eager to be a part of Seven Poplars again. Then she meets Daniel Brown and her world turns topsy-turvy. Does she belong in Delaware with her family, or half a world away, serving God as a Mennonite missionary's wife?

And if she follows her heart and chooses Daniel, will it tear her traditional family apart?

Wishing you peace and joy,

Emma Miller

Questions for Discussion

1. Do you think Anna should have allowed Samuel into the house with only Susanna as a chaperone? Why or why not?

2. Should Samuel have asked Hannah's permission to court Anna before bringing the matter up with Anna? Do you think the fact that the community believed he was interested in courting Hannah should have affected his decision?

3. Do you think Dorcas had Anna's best interests at heart when she cautioned Anna against considering allowing Samuel to court her? Were Dorcas's concerns reasonable? Accurate? Do you think Dorcas was motivated by jealousy toward her friend?

4. Was it fair for Samuel to ask Anna, at her young age, to even consider becoming his wife and mother to five children? Do you think a woman her age could be the mother to another woman's children? Is it possible for a woman of any age to love another woman's children as if they were truly her own? Is Anna ready to take on such a huge responsibility?

5. How would you have handled Peter and Rudy's mischief-making with Martha? Do you think Samuel handled the situation well? How would you have responded if you were their parent? If you were Martha? Do you believe Anna will change Samuel's way of disciplining the children?

6. Why do you think Grossmama treated Hannah the way she did? Why was Anna able to see past Grossmama's grumpiness? Have you ever dealt with someone like Grossmama? How did you respond?

7. Do you see Samuel as the "catch" that everyone else in the county does? Why or why not? Do you think he and Anna are well-suited to each other?

8. Why do you think Peter and Rudy treated Anna badly, when Samuel's girls took an immediate liking to her? What did you think about the way she handled their animosity toward her? Do you believe that Anna will ever be able to fill a mother's role in their hearts?

9. Do you think Samuel was rushing Anna's decision concerning courting and marrying him? Would it have made a difference in their relationship if he had given her more time? How

much time is enough time to decide if you're in love with someone and want to spend the rest of your life with him?

10. Do you think that Anna could have become Samuel's wife and the children's mother without a change of heart concerning herself? When in your life have you needed to change your opinion of yourself? Why is it so difficult for women to accept and value themselves?

LARGER-PRINT BOOKS!

GET 2 FREE LARGER-PRINT NOVELS PLUS 2 FREE MYSTERY GIFTS

Love Inspired®

Larger-print novels are now available...

YES! Please send me 2 FREE LARGER-PRINT Love Inspired® novels and my 2 FREE mystery gifts (gifts are worth about $10). After receiving them, if I don't wish to receive any more books, I can return the shipping statement marked "cancel". If I don't cancel, I will receive 6 brand-new novels every month and be billed just $4.99 per book in the U.S. or $5.49 per book in Canada. That's a saving of at least 23% off the cover price. It's quite a bargain! Shipping and handling is just 50¢ per book in the U.S. and 75¢ per book in Canada.* I understand that accepting the 2 free books and gifts places me under no obligation to buy anything. I can always return a shipment and cancel at any time. Even if I never buy another book, the two free books and gifts are mine to keep forever.

122/322 IDN FEG3

Name _____ (PLEASE PRINT)

Address _____ Apt. #

City _____ State/Prov. _____ Zip/Postal Code

Signature (if under 18, a parent or guardian must sign)

Mail to the **Reader Service**:
IN U.S.A.: P.O. Box 1867, Buffalo, NY 14240-1867
IN CANADA: P.O. Box 609, Fort Erie, Ontario L2A 5X3

Not valid to current subscribers to Love Inspired Larger-Print books.

**Are you a current subscriber to Love Inspired books and want to receive the larger-print edition?
Call 1-800-873-8635 or visit www.ReaderService.com.**

* Terms and prices subject to change without notice. Prices do not include applicable taxes. Sales tax applicable in N.Y. Canadian residents will be charged applicable taxes. Offer not valid in Quebec. This offer is limited to one order per household. All orders subject to credit approval. Credit or debit balances in a customer's account(s) may be offset by any other outstanding balance owed by or to the customer. Please allow 4 to 6 weeks for delivery. Offer available while quantities last.

Your Privacy—The Reader Service is committed to protecting your privacy. Our Privacy Policy is available online at www.ReaderService.com or upon request from the Reader Service.

We make a portion of our mailing list available to reputable third parties that offer products we believe may interest you. If you prefer that we not exchange your name with third parties, or if you wish to clarify or modify your communication preferences, please visit us at www.ReaderService.com/consumerchoice or write to us at Reader Service Preference Service, P.O. Box 9062, Buffalo, NY 14269. Include your complete name and address.

LILP11B